A Rotten Girl

J. Ursula Topaz

Copyright © 2024 Jemma Topaz

All rights reserved

A Rotten Girl is a work of fiction. Names, characters, places, and incidents are the products of the author's imagination or are used fictitiously. Any resemblance to actual events, locales, or persons, living or dead, is entirely coincidental.

The moral right of the author has been asserted.

Except for short excerpts for the purposes of review or commentary, no part of this publication may be reproduced, stored or introduced into a retrieval system, or transmitted, in any form or by any means (electronic, mechanical, photocopying, recording or otherwise), without the prior written permission of the copyright owner.

Cover by Benjanun Sriduangkaew.

To Amelia, Angelica, Carmilla and Celeste;
For adventures past and future.

Table of Contents

Table of Contents 5

Epigraph 7

Chapter One: Normal Lies. 9

Chapter Two: Detransition, Maybe. 21

Chapter Three: First Scars. 37

Chapter Four: Don't Tell. 53

Chapter Five: Cover Reveal. 69

Chapter Six: Being Noticed. 83

Chapter Seven: Consonance, Perhaps. 101

Chapter Eight: Conventional Romance. 117

Chapter Nine: Questionable Characters. 133

Chapter Ten: Rotten Girl. 149

Chapter Eleven: The End. 167

Acknowledgements 179

Other Books by this Author 180

"The fujoshi have much wisdom, but have failed to cultivate a sense of morality."

~ Halimede
(@halimedeMF on Twitter/X)

Chapter One: Normal Lies.

The first line of a novel is critical; this is a truth universally acknowledged. Awakening one morning from uneasy dreams to find the clocks striking thirteen; returning to Manderley, again, upon the death of Marley.

So why couldn't I find a good way to introduce Peter and Robb?

Now, don't worry. I haven't written my book in order; I am not stuck on the first line. I'm not serialising it on AO3. I had a proper plan. Later sections were at least drafted, except the end. And the start; the problem was that my plan said "1. P & R meet-cute" but life, my life, mostly did meet-prosaics.

(And yes, I am inspired by life. I am picturing you here as the interviewer from a literary romance magazine, quite an upgrade from the reality of being a solitary mental critic. A constant and unfickle reader, who unfortunately never spends any money, or bigs me up on Twitter. Anyway, yes, I am inspired by life, you see; the subtle interplay of moods and motivations that far surpass any machinations of fiction. I would probably laugh or sip my wine here, if that was real, or I had wine.)

The truth is that Barbs and I fucked on our first meeting. We weren't even in love, yet, we just thought, "might as well." I mean, I realise that we were not helping the whole trans girls are total sluts thing, but Shrewsbury to London cost ninety quid return, and it wasn't worth two or three trips to discover we are not compatible.

Oh, we were attracted to each other, certainly. Barbs was a very handsome butch; clockable, but that's less important to butches, isn't it? And she found me a passable femme, I guess. We shared a pizza and then went back to my place. No hilarious misunderstandings at all. "Do you want to fuck?" she said.

We hadn't even lied more than usual over Discord; Barbs was more a switch than a top, but she pretended well. I had several months to go before I would actually admit to taking my name from *Steven Universe*. Pearl was an excellent character! You know, normal lies. If only one of us was secretly an assassin or a member of the royal family; that would be much easier.

A young prince and a grizzled assassin; that was Paul Sisters' debut novel. *Muzzle and Escutcheon*. Well, a noble scion and a grizzled contractor; that's more 'realistic' than a prince and an assassin. As a Brit I know the secret of our monarchy; they are deeply unfuckable. Honestly, I was going to do a huge thing here about my rivalry with Paul— a dashing cis gay author about town—and myself—not gay, not cis, not a fucking bloke. Not really about town. But I couldn't be arsed, especially for you; I am Paul.

Chapter One: Normal Lies.

I am not Paul, of course. It—he—is my *nom de plume*, or maybe *nom de guerre*. He has people keen to read him, that's the biggest difference.

My first proper novel—by me, that is, not Paul—was stunning. Personal and honest, joyous and mournful, bittersweet and elegiac. A heartfelt examination of what it was like to grow up trans in this grey and rain-swept island.

It had sunk without a trace.

The book, not the island. Unfortunately.

Oh, a few trans girls read it. But when fifty percent of your audience is named Emily or Zoe, that's a bad sign. The small press that finally published it went out of business shortly thereafter.

"That wasn't entirely your fault, Pearl," my agent had said. Well, typed. I had never actually met Beatrice. "They were rather incompetent, even for a small press," she continued. "But your book's Titanic reenactment didn't help. I really thought your story would have broader appeal, you know, connect to normal people. But the market must have shifted. Perhaps if you'd made it more miserable, that would have hit the mark."

"It was drawn from real experience," I explained, again. "It has precisely the level of misery of my actual life. Which is more than I'd like, but is not infinite."

"Right," said Beatrice. "I'm just saying that if the protagonist got beaten up more, that would probably sell better. Maybe she could have fallen for her bully? Gritty but spicy. She mends his transphobia; that would have been a good ending, right? You could write about how you shouldn't be transphobic."

"Inspiring," I said. "Maybe we can get J.K. to blurb?"

"Oh, I don't think—ah, you're mocking me?" said Beatrice.

"A bit."

"Well, you're the author," she said. "I'm just trying to teach you the realities of the market. Bring me something that will sell. Maybe to a demographic that has money."

Really, Beatrice was the perfect agent. I was not entirely convinced that she could read. She didn't do nuance or subtlety. Or sensitivity. She didn't need any of that nonsense. She could intuit The Market; map out its dark and writhing tentacles. Divine whether it would like a particular offering. Like a holy idiot savant. Oh, she could get caught out when it suddenly changed its shape; it was not rational, after all—it was one of those ancient and terrible gods. Eldritch and squamous. And racist, come to think of it. But she was a dedicated priestess. Also, no-one else wanted to be my agent.

I had used to be a nonbeliever; I had proudly declared my independence from The Market. I would write what I want; queer and authentic. I had come up through the ranks of fanfic and Scribblehub porn; I did not care about not being read. Writing is not about reading, after all.

Beatrice had tolerated this. Humoured me. Her belief in The Market was not some fickle thing; she was not defensive at my dismissal of her faith. She sighed and smiled at my intransigence. She knew The Market was just

Chapter One: Normal Lies.

toying with me; that my long-legged freedom was just it letting me use up all my energy before it struck, enveloping me in ink-black tentacles.

The big problem about being authentic is—

There is something hard to explain about putting yourself—in book form—out there. Oh, a fictionalised me, and a fictionalised life, but me in the important ways. To dissect your faults and your foibles, to anatomize your desires and dreams, and to present that to the world. And for the world to go, "Meh."

It was in that breath, that meh, that Paul was born. He would perform obeisance to the Market. He would write something that would sell. I wanted to be read. I wanted to actually make money. Paul would hunt fujoshi.

Fujoshi (lit. "rotten girls") were female fans of M/M romance. Romance and sex. Started in manga but had now spread to boring novels too.

Cishet white women, in particular; that was the demographic he—I—was targeting. Oh, I'm generalising, of course. Or rather, Paul was. What do straight cis women want? Gay men, making out.

Why? Gentle reader, that is a subject for someone who cares. Some think that in fiction about hot gay men they can find safety. A world in which they won't be objectified or worse. True, this is often because they don't really exist in this gay and womanless fictional world. All romances aimed at male-attracted women are like that to some degree; coping with the fact that the demographic they're into wants to rape and murder them. Their own absence makes them safe.

Of course, sometimes they just want be the ones doing the objectifying. They've earned it, after all. Maybe it's a chance to punish men; these books sometimes contain abuse that the characters need saving from.

Some even suggest it is a dagger aimed at the heart of patriarchy. As they are actively sexualizing the male form, they say, this puts them in a position of power over men.

I don't know; I just know that gay dudes and straight chicks go together like children and clergy.

I developed Paul like every other character. He's mid-twenties, light brown hair, dark brown eyes. White, of course. It's possible that ethnically ambiguous might be a better choice, but I go with the safety of pallor. Paul is a twink, becoming aware of the existence of twink death. He works out, but just to stay toned; he doesn't want to get jacked. He's single; his love life is a disaster.

He has his own Instagram account where he regrams celebrity and microcelebrity gay folks, when I remember to. His Twitter account is better used; he often does capsule reviews of books about marginalised people. I've only used him once or twice to criticise, subtly, acquaintances' books. But much more often to praise them.

Then, more recently, his Twitter has begun to refer to his new book; a stock image of a typewriter or a cup of coffee, and, "final chapter going well," or, "asking my agent how hot I'm allowed to make the sex scenes." We

Chapter One: Normal Lies.

don't follow each other though, maybe out of paranoia, but I retweet Paul's tweets, sometimes with an, "Excited!!". We are fellow marginalised writers, after all. It's only the degree of fellowship that I'm lying about.

Perhaps the writer (I say to myself, testing a *bon mot* for pithiness) should be themselves an exercise of writing. Or *exorcism in writing*, would that be better?

Barbs had put down a cup of tea, spilling it over the edge of the mug. She had filled the mug too high, as usual; she used the sleeve of her jumper to remove the spillage.

I sighed and moved the laptop away. Barbs works with computers, but the kind of computers with beige boxes and separate keyboards. The sort of keyboard that would probably survive being dunked in Tetley, and if it somehow doesn't, well, just pick another from the skip. She doesn't understand why I have a laptop that, if exposed to the vicissitudes of everyday life, will throw a fit, and require a sniffy 'technician' to charge me virtually the same cost as a new one.

"How's it going?" Barbs asked. Her voice was low, both in volume and pitch.

"I wasn't just staring blankly off into space," I said, needlessly defensive. "Okay, yes, I was, but you know."

We are in my bedroom, in the flat that I rent. Well, my mother actually pays for most of it. It's quiet, so my roommate must be out.

"Hey, my job requires staring off into space, too," said Barbs. "In the IT industry, we call it 'thinking'."

I chuckled. "That won't catch on in the world of authors. Cogitating, maybe. Brooding. Woolgathering."

"Woolgathering?"

"You don't see it much nowadays," I said. I was barely thirty; I'm not sure why I talk like this. "It means daydreaming, idle fancies. People used to gather tufts of wool from bushes and fences. It wasn't a very productive or profitable line of work. But I suppose the idea is that you might gather enough thoughts for a, like, metaphorical mitten."

"If it was unprofitable," said Barbs. "But people did it anyway, doesn't that mean that they didn't have much choice? It ought to mean, you know, anxious precarity, not fanciful daydreaming."

Okay, don't think badly of me, but I sometimes forget that Barbs has a brain. She's a butch, so I don't always recall that fact.

"At any rate," I said, "I haven't gathered enough tufts to make up a suitable meet-cute. Probably because I only ever had meet-prosaics." Yes, I am repeating myself here, but I wanted the chance for someone other than me to hear it.

"What about ours?" said Barbs.

"Ours was the epitome of prosaic," I said. "A shared *pizza quattro stagioni*, an invitation here, and then heavy frotting. Not useful. I mean great, obviously, but not useful to a writer."

Chapter One: Normal Lies.

"Wow," said Barbs. "But I meant our first real meeting."

"Huh?"

"I told you about it," said Barbs. "Our impromptu transatlantic transgender girl film club had finished watching D.E.B.S., remember?"

"Sort of."

"Pretty much everyone had logged off the Discord voice channel," she said. "But I was doing a bit of coding on another tab, and I couldn't be bothered right away."

"And I thought I had," I said. "But I must have just minimised it or something stupid."

"You were in a hurry, because you were getting a call," said Barbs.

"Right. My bloody dad."

"It confused me when I heard you talking," said Barbs. "You know, autistic sound processing stuff."

"Plus I was using my boy-voice."

"Yeah, that too," she continued. "It took me longer than it should have to realise you weren't talking to me. But, instead, I was listening to a personal call. Of course, what I should have done was exit the channel. But I was anxious about you hearing the departure tone and somehow blaming me for eavesdropping. Even then I fancied you, so I didn't want to get caught as a creepy spy. But the longer the call went on, the more impossible exiting unnoticed seemed. I would have to hope that you would wander off or something, when the call was done."

A Rotten Girl

"Right, and like all calls with my dad, it got worse and worse," I said. "Yes, I was still trying to be a writer. No, no bites yet. Yes, I am no John Grisham. And on and on. Eventually, it was; *Are you still doing that genderfluid crap?* And I was cross, so I finally told him; No, I've been on HRT for four years, and I am definitely a girl now."

"And I hissed, 'Yes!'," said Barbs. "I didn't mean to; it just came out. I thought you'd be cross."

"I was just happy not to be alone," I said. "You comforted me, and we talked for hours."

"Yes," said Barbs. "Though it wasn't the first time we'd talked, it was the first time we actually *talked* talked, you know. The first time we really met."

"Right," I said. "Yes. That's good."

The gun was small; a Seecamp's LWS 380. Machined metal and black oil. It was strapped to Robb's muscular calf, beneath the black trousers. He would have preferred a bigger gun, but that wouldn't have made it through security. Robb put his leg up on a vacuum cleaner, and retrieved the gun; he checked the slide, the magazine, the safety, and then put the weapon in his pocket. The plan was simple; identify Sheikh Al Sakhif and put at least three bullets through his skull. Escaping was a longer plan.

Robb straightened his waiter's jacket, sized specially to fit over his muscled frame, and prepared to exit this broom closet. But as he went for the door, the handle turned.

Chapter One: Normal Lies.

Lord Peter Ukebridge-Talbot—son of the Duke of Glearbury—was slightly built, elfin, with pale skin and soft blue eyes. Eyes which were close to tears, Robb saw from the darkened corner into which he had quickly retreated.

"I am listening, father." Lord Peter was speaking into a mobile phone. "But you're not listening to me."

There was a pause while the other end of the phone call shouted.

"No, I will not marry Cecelia," said Peter. "Father, this is my life, after all."

Robb was expressly forbidden from shooting any nobility other than his target. His boss, Mr Herald, had been very clear on that point. Fellow waitstaff, functionaries, administrators; if necessary or convenient those could be killed. But Robb's boss didn't want him to kill anyone of the notable class. At any rate, Robb was not going to kill Peter; first, his gun was unsilenced, and second, something about that delicate but sharp jawline made him want to...

"I mean, it shouldn't be that hard to understand?" Peter continued, voice a shaky whisper. "It is not the 1900s. I do not care if people say that. Why won't you accept that... father, I'm gay."

"Yes!" muttered Robb. Not even loud enough to be a whisper, but Peter's head whipped towards Robb's hiding place.

Lord Peter shut the phone case. "Who's there?" he said, tremulously.

Chapter Two: Detransition, Maybe.

Two and a half thousand words is a little on the short side for a chapter. I mean, it's fine. There are no actual rules on chapter size; no patron saint of writers is going to bonk me on the head for pissing in the august halls of authors. But I try to aim for at least three and a half thousand.

I contemplated expanding a couple of paragraphs, but my 'style' is already discursive enough. Instead, I closed the laptop and took my headphones off. The dull warbling of terrible music became louder. I wandered out into the living room.

"Oh yay," said Pippin. "Are you taking a break? Can I turn it up now?"

I rolled my eyes, but in a friendly way, and nodded. I padded through to the kitchen part of the room, and popped a couple of slices into the toaster.

I am deeply annoyed at Pippin watching *Eurovision*; firstly, because my tolerance for badly translated ballads is very low, and secondly because, well, it's a bit trite, isn't it? Introducing my gay roommate yelling and sofa dancing to terrible Euro-pop; why don't I just go the whole hog and describe him receiving anal sex in a really camp way?

And it's not like I don't have a choice; *Eurovision* is too bloody long, but I've known him for a couple of years, and only a small percentage of that has been marked by pop stars in lamé leotards. Still, all those other times aren't where I want to start, and I am nothing if not a reliable narrator.

I've no idea how he actually has sex, by the way, other than loudly. Maybe he doesn't do anal.

"Watch it with me?" said Pippin. "It feels a bit stupid watching it alone." He turned the volume down while the presenters did one of their 'hilarious skits'.

"Sure, for a bit," I said. "Why aren't you watching it with Dean?"

"He's watching it with his wife," Pippin said, glumly. "And their friends."

"Ah, sorry." Pippin has the sort of hyper-specific taste in boyfriends that you can only afford when you're a supernaturally handsome twink. He says he likes 'dad bods' but really he just likes dads. Closeted dads who are beginning to come to terms with the fact that they are not as straight as they pretend. I don't judge. Well, I do judge, but mostly because of the 'sleeping with men' thing; the exact flavour of man does not bother me. I'm not homophobic, obviously, I'm just surprised people don't have more taste.

"Straight people shouldn't be allowed to watch *Eurovision*," Pippin said. "It's basically appropriation. You don't see me watching whatever *Top Gear* is called now."

Chapter Two: Detransition, Maybe.

"I don't think you see anyone watching that," I said. I took my toast and joined him on the sofa.

"So, yeah, I was going to stay in my room, and have a bit of a cry, do some moping," said Pippin. "But I got bored, so..."

"Okay, but your other friends," I said, "they must be having gatherings."

"I've already told them I was going to be moping," Pippin said. "I can't turn up now, *not* devastatingly sad. People will think I'm shallow." He sighed. "Pearl, do you think I've got a limited emotional range because I get bored too easily? I feel emotions fine, but then, like, I'm supposed to continue feeling them? For how long?"

"Well—" I began.

"Ooh, they're back!" squealed Pippin, and turned the sound up. I ate my toast.

Obviously, you might have detected some more inspiration here; some of Paul, my imaginary author, was influenced by Pippin. I had to be careful that I didn't stumble into stereotype territory though; Paul is much more sensible than Pippin.

It's always a difficult one; the difference between signs of membership, and just stereotypes. For example; most transfems love *Fallout: New Vegas*, and *Undertale*. I don't play computer games, and for a while I was worried that I was a bad tran because of it. In the early post-egg phase, as a trans hatchling, I would actually pretend; "Oh, Benny, yeah! What a character," or, "Sans, gosh. Talk about... a person?" But I got better. Okay, what I actually got was a blåhaj, but it's the same principle.

Pippin is actually pretty good as a roommate; he's fairly tidy and very hygienic. He doesn't steal your food. He's generous with his weed. He likes bad telly, though, and leaves it on whatever he's doing. He doesn't really read books, which is not a Paul characteristic, for obvious reasons. Yes, Pippin did choose his name from *The Lord of the Rings*, but the films, not the books. Still Pippin was a useful fallback when I needed a character touch for Paul's twitter.

The one thing that might trip me up—in the deceit that Paul is a real person—is the fact I'm a writer. The difference between characters and people is that characters make sense. If I ask Pippin why he likes Eurovision, I'd get that "It's fun and dance-y," or some such. If I ask Paul then...

It was that winter that my grandfather decided that he would abandon the world of the audiophile. Or rather, saw that the world was closing to him. His shaking had become worse; he couldn't place the needle with any precision. He even dropped Kind of Blue while removing it from its sleeve. It shattered into two pieces, like his life before and after the illness.

My grandfather turned, with disgust at both his frailty and the world, to streaming services. And I inherited his record player, and his collection.

Chapter Two: Detransition, Maybe.

He was a man of eclectic tastes, or maybe of tastes too refined for mundane people. Classical, jazz, pop; it was all thrown in there. My grandfather liked music, full stop. I didn't have his broadness of taste; I liked the pop. In my attic room, that winter, I felt the sun of Rome, Eurovision 1991. Something of that bright but long gone sound resonated with the newfound feelings of my teenage body.

Or some such. Obviously, I'd have to do some research; I doubt Eurovision '91 was actually in Italy, but you get the idea. In real life, you get maybe two personality-building anecdotes; any more and you'll annoy people. Three, if you're famous. In fiction, if you mention it, then it should have some meaning; even if that meaning is just to establish verisimilitude. Why did I choose *Kind of Blue* as the album that got smashed? Maybe my father had a lot of Miles Davis on CDs that he would play while he was in one of his moods. Or maybe it's a reference to the bloody *curtains are blue* meme.

So I am careful not to overwrite Paul.

I finished my toast, and logged onto Paul's twitter account: "I'm on the final straight (ha) of my book, so not listening to Eurovision myself, but bigging up all the fans! #eurovisable."

Beatrice had been oddly encouraging when I explained my plan to use a false name.

"Oh yes," she had messaged. "Detransitioning. Very in right now."

"No, just a pseudonym," I said. "I'm still... you know what, doesn't matter. It's just a pen name."

"Authors are all pseudonyms to me, Paul," she said. "Pearl Camellia wasn't real either, was she?" Camellia was a made-up surname; my real one, Campbell, was boring, and anyway, girls prefer not to be doxed.

"It's a great idea," continued Beatrice. "Men connect to the reader much more directly. Are you still a lesbian?"

"I am," I said. "But Paul is not; he's gay."

"Excellent!" said Beatrice. "I suppose it makes sense; as a woman you used to like women, so now you've untransitioned to a man, you like men."

"Beatrice, I don't want to be rude, but are you drunk?"

"Paul, I work with writers every day," she said. "Naturally I drink."

I suppose it was good that Paul was not my deadname. That would have really fucked me up. I had chosen it because it was close to Pearl. Sort of.

***

Pippin was very good at rolling joints; he was a stoner before he was a boy, he says. That is the sort of joke you only really make in front of other trans people, because there's always a danger of some cis saying, "But didn't you say you were always a whatever, eh, eh?" And the answer for a lot of trans people is yes, but it's easier sometimes to speak of, "When I was a man." So much of life is presentation, after all.

"Where's Barbara?" Pippin asked, passing me the joint.

Chapter Two: Detransition, Maybe.

"Manchester," I said. Another good thing about Pippin is that he doesn't object to Barbs staying here when she's in this part of the country. She's a contractor, in IT, and it takes her up and down the UK. She has to boymode through it all, of course. Aside from the actual danger, she says she really couldn't bear having to come out over and over again. And look, we prefer allies to enemies, of course, but they are annoying. *What's the difference between drag and being transgender? Or is it transexual? Why don't you look like Hunter Schafer? We think our cat's a tranny… oh, can't I say that? Are you sure? I'm an ally, so it's reclaiming.*

"Manchester's cool," said Pippin. The telly was showing YouTube; we had started watching past Eurovisions, got into Tom Scott attending Eurovision, and we were now on him talking about lifts that go sideways.

"I've not been," I said. I wondered about posting as Paul, stoned. Nah, I decided, too easy to blow my cover. Misgender myself. Well, mismisgender myself. I passed the joint back.

"So, your next book's almost done?" said Pippin, after a pause that I was no longer able to estimate the length of.

"Yeah, a few last bits to write; an early encounter I haven't completely decided the shape of. But pretty much," I said.

"Cool," said Pippin. "I told my friends about your last book."

"Really?"

"Yeah," he said. "Well, I couldn't remember, like, the full name, but I told them it had 'tattoo' in the title."

"Great." I sighed.

"Do you think there are a lot of books like that?"

"A few, yeah," I said. "For future reference: *Transient Tattoo, a novel about the impermanence of modern life on the margins.*"

"Girl," he said, "I am never going to remember that."

"Fair," I said. "No-one does."

Pippin passed the joint back, and cuddled up to me. He always got affectionate when high. I tasted his saliva on the joint. I think that if Pippin and I had been cis, we'd have probably fucked at least once, even though we are definitely not each other's type.

I've always taken the view that being a lesbian was about not centering men in your life, your romance, or your sexuality. Yes, certainly, not sleeping with men is a big part of that, but also in refusing, as far as you can, to buy into the heteronormative phantasm they promote. People do not universally agree with me on this. Some say lesbianism is about reacting to the idea of a penis by jumping on a chair in the manner of a 50s housewife. This is not a popular view in the transbian community, for obvious reasons. Others treat it like a religion, the Order of Saint Lezzy, where you are expected to police yourself for signs of heresy. For example: do you ever fancy a beautiful and feminine but sadly male celebrity? *Sin.* Did you check out that butch's arse only for him to turn around and not be a butch? *Exile.* Taken to its logical conclusion, this

Chapter Two: Detransition, Maybe.

would make lesbianism a purely posthumous condition, known only to the creator. After all, that girl you kissed and lost touch with? *For all you know, he might, sometime down the line, have had a crisis of gender, and now be a man.* According to the followers of this religion, this means you were unknowingly bisexual for most of your life. God's going to laugh in your face, when you get to lesbian heaven.

So, yeah, I prefer the 'don't centre men' idea, but not everyone agrees. I received a Goodreads review of *Transient Tattoo*, for example:

Until at least a third of the way through Camellia's debut novel, I believed it had a speculative setting; an alternative present where man did not exist. A rather rambly addition to the gendercide genre. But when the protagonist's father turns up, I realise that Camillia just doesn't want to write men, or maybe can't write men. The father is a cypher, barely characterised at all. If the sexes were reversed, and women subjected to this marginalisation, you can bet that Pearl Camellia and her ilk would be objecting...

This at least got a dozen retweets on my, "Yes, what about the men?" post. Twitter name The-Hated-Authortrix retweeted with, "I regret to announce that the men are at it again," and got several times as many.

So my dislike of men is on the record. If lesbians had cards, I'd be a card-carrying member. But an impeccable twink, with just enough weed in the air? Maybe. If I was cis.

A Rotten Girl

I can't really speak for Pippin, but he seems like a very committed dadosexual. Still, I've caught what might be the occasional glance. If we were cis, then our mild attraction would be easy to explain; it's not uncommon for one's demographic of attraction to be slightly blurred; like a sexy chromatic aberration, at its very edge. From certain angles, Pippin looks like a petite butch. Conversely, with enough weed goggles in place, I probably look slightly dadish.

Which is, of course, the reason why we will never sleep together. I will never be one hundred percent sure that I am not reacting to the ghost of genders past; that some stupid, primitive part of my brain is not misgendering him, and is attracted to the result. And conversely, of course, that he might be seeing the abandoned boy-me, reflected in my slightly dad-like body. Gender necromancy. This is not true, of course, probably, but it's enough to stop us.

As an aside: here is the secret about being a Twitter trans (obviously, you already know, you're in my head, dear reader, but somehow I imagine you as cis/clueless); you do not ever express doubts about transition. When you're a new tran online, among all the encouragement, a middle-ranked tran will sidle up to you, press a knife against your ribs and hiss that rule at you.

It makes sense; cis men, for example, do they ever worry about whether they're really a man? Most will react in anger if you question that. Cis women, much the same.

Chapter Two: Detransition, Maybe.

So, trans women should have the same certainty. And we do, eventually, but for many of us, it takes a little while. As a new hatchling, you're wondering if you're screwing your life up for nothing, you're wondering if you will have to deal with people looking at you in *that* way forever. And what's the point, you think, if you don't pass?

The principal argument of anti-trans idiots is, "you're a man," (usually to both trans women and trans men, because they are not bright). Explaining that 'Biology 101' isn't actually the final word in biology: "you're a man." Leader caught looking at teen rape fiction: "you're a man." Noting that there are a remarkable number of evangelists, incels and nazis standing shoulder-to-shoulder with their 'feminist' cause: "you're a man." It is their ultimate argument, which you might think would be affected by (a) not actually being an argument, and (b) never remotely working. Also, (c) spelling "you're" as "your" half of the time. But their cult is only loosely aware of reason.

So you can see why the High Council of Transfems does not want any newbie responding to, "You're a man," with, "Am I? I don't think so, but I'm not completely sure..."

This can lead to an annoying kind of policing. Express a worry that your family won't support you; *but they might, mine did!* Worry that your friends will shun you; *give them an opportunity to prove their friendship.* Concerned that your job will fire you; *actually, that's probably illegal.* Think that being trans will be hard; *it's actually easy, maybe you're just bad at it.*

The prevailing attitude towards trans girls is so negative, that even toxic positivity seems like an improvement.

Of course, in the end you work out that being a woman isn't the problem, and that being trans also isn't the problem. Spoiler: the problem is transphobia.

(And also, you will realise cis men and cis women are often not as secure in their gender as you, a confused egg, thought.)

I passed the joint back, and cursed transphobia. Tom Scott was in a centrifuge. (Not because of transphobia; he just does that.)

***

Robb made his way through the stables like he belonged there; in fact, he had memorised floor plans and pictures long into the night. He nodded at the other grooms and servants, touched his caps to the rich folk, and was gruffly friendly to the horses. Despite his size and build, Robb was surprisingly adept at impersonation; an easy confidence will get you a long way.

His employers believed their enemy would strike here; a small and expensive country lodge, completely bought out for a fox hunt. Mr Herald was adamant that Robb was only here to observe; to gather intel on a competitor. It wasn't going to be easy, especially since he couldn't pretend to be one of the guests or one of the hotel staff; the group was too small, everyone knew each other. The outdoors staff at least were

Chapter Two: Detransition, Maybe.

ignored; the staff belonging to the nobles thought he worked for the lodge, and vice versa. Security was tight though, which meant it was just as well that Robb was unarmed.

He left the stables, and stepped around a corner. He could see into the lodge through the French windows; the dinner was in full swing. Informal and rustic to these people; impossibly posh to a man of Robb's class. Carefully he made his way round to the darker side of the building. He made use of the decorative edging to climb up and grab a second-storey window ledge; going by the pictures, this window was usually open. The morning staff often smoked out of it. Of course, it was closed now, but it raised easily on its sashes. Not locked, and the alarm had been messed with; smokers were the assassin's best friend. From the faint smell it was weed rather than straight tobacco; Robb supposed that even expensive country lodges must move with the times.

Robb found himself in a staff utility room; it was mostly used in the mornings when changing linens and tidying, though he wasn't completely safe here.

He heard some shouting from downstairs, then a number of crashes. Robb opened the door a fraction and peered out. No sign of anyone, but a thin green smoke crept along the floor. Robb closed the door, quietly but hurriedly. He recognised the scent; knockout gas. Even this minor exposure had him feeling a little woozy.

He used the staff sink to wet a pillowcase, and fashioned it into an improvised mask.

A Rotten Girl

He ventured out; the gas was already thicker, but it seemed to be drifting up from downstairs. He crouched and moved towards the stairwell. Robb had to descend to the first landing to see what was happening. The banqueting room was full of smoke, but he saw three figures moving around. Gas masks. Women, going by the silhouettes and the voices.

"Any sign of him?" asked one.

"Not this one," said another.

"Or this one," said a third.

"We're running out of time," said the first. "He has to be somewhere in the building."

Robb backed up; their next step was clear. A door opened on his left; a young man, unsteady on his feet.

"Wha—" the man said.

Robb grabbed him, clamped a hand over his mouth, and bundled him back into the room. He carefully closed the door.

"I say—" said the young man, before Robb put his hand over his mouth again.

Robb realised that he knew him: Lord Peter Ukebridge-Talbot. Awkward.

"People are coming to kill you," said Robb, looking around. "Or maybe kidnap. Don't make it easy for them."

Lord Peter tried to form words, but then gave up. Unsurprisingly, Peter seemed increasingly groggy; he was almost slumped against Robb's body. He was so delicate, thought Robb, precious and birdlike.

Chapter Two: Detransition, Maybe.

Robb looked around the room. He would give the window a try if Peter had been conscious. The wardrobe was a possibility, as was under the bed. Which was more obvious? Robb sighed, and chose at random.

He would have to congratulate the lodge staff, thought Robb; the underside of the bed frame was impressively dust free. He held Peter against him, hand still over his mouth, to guard against snoring. Robb's muscular chest barely fit under the bed; he could scarcely believe that Peter was the same species as him. So frail and beautiful; maybe the rich really were different. Robb felt sleepy; with alarm, he realised that his makeshift mask was virtually dry.

The door opened, and someone entered. A pause; Robb held his breath, and prayed that Peter stayed quiet.

The figure made an annoyed sound, and exited the room. Robb breathed again, and was unable to stop himself drifting off, holding Peter close.

Chapter Three: First Scars.

Hardly anyone writes, "The End," at the end of their book. In the worst case, your readers will figure it out when the words stop. Ideally, you've put in some sort of denouement so that they do not assume that a small meteorite has hit you, and you have then, in your last moments of life, hit the publish button. Ending your book with, "The End," is a newbie move.

I did write, "The End," with a flourish. And then deleted it.

"Done," I announced.

Barbs looked up blearily from my bed. "The book?" she asked. It was still quite early in the morning, but I had awoken at dawn thinking about grammar, and knowing I would be free soon.

"Yep, final rewriting," I said, "and another final spelling and grammar check. There will still be loads wrong with it, but good enough to send it to Beatrice."

"Can I read it?" asked Barbs.

"Um, no. Not yet. It won't be your kind of thing."

"I loved *Transient Tattoo*," she said. That was the problem, *Muzzle and Escutcheon* was not for fans of *Transient Tattoo*. In fact, it was a reverse comp; if you enjoyed this book, then for fuck's sake don't check out M&E.

"Thank you," I said. "But I'm a bit insecure at the moment."

"Send it off," said Barbs. "And come back to bed. I will make you feel secure."

I typed up the email, then my hand hovered over the send button. I tried to imagine the email arriving.

Beatrice had sounds turned off, but caught a glance of the notification as it flickered in the corner of the screen. She sighed, I guessed, and flipped her printer on. She seems like the sort to use hard copy.

While the printer was going, she stood up, stretched her arms, and looked out over the city. A vodka bottle stands on the desk; she pours a measure into her mug. Beatrice is middle-aged, and a little worn-looking, tired.

Her office is reasonably sized. Watercolours of English country scenes hang on the wall. Her husband paints them; they are just okay.

When the printer chimes to signal it has finished, Beatrice settles down at her desk to read it. She has a red biro, even though she is not an editor.

Hmm. Do agents have offices? Or printers?

Her computer warbled, unheard in Beatrice's cubicle. Beatrice had headphones in place; everyone did, otherwise it was too noisy. This Beatrice was an ex-goth, aged out of torn fishnets and ripped tee-shirts, but her dark clothes still bore a trace of that style.

Chapter Three: First Scars.

She got to my email eventually and opened up the text. She skimmed a couple of pages, then began putting together a list.

"What are you doing?" asked Barbs. She propped herself up on one arm.

"Oh... imagining what it will be like when Beatrice gets my email."

"Have you sent the email?" said Barb.

"No," I admitted.

"Do you actually know enough about her to have any idea what she's going to do with it?"

"Well, no," I admitted, again. "But I can make a reasonable guess, based on logic—"

Barbs collapsed back. "Send the email, and come to bed."

The email hit the router and was transferred to the uplink, a high-intensity laser transmitting into Beatrice's orbital station, The Beahive.

A tiny light appeared on a curved console of glittering colours. Beatrice touched it; the illumination bouncing off her silver bodysuit. The glowing dot expanded into charts and graphs. Beatrice nodded to herself, and flicked the light towards another cluster.

She pushed from the desk, and turned towards her harem. Seven men and three women stood nude, aside from collars.

"Yuri futures are up," Beatrice notes dispassionately, and gestures at one of the men. A multiplicity of arms descend from the ceiling, enclosing him. When they withdraw, their subject is another, slightly confused, woman.

"Good," said Beatrice, again to herself. "Got to stay on top of the demographic."

"Get out of your mind palace," said Barbs, "and hit the button!"

Mother Beatrice surveyed the Hall of Scribes. She had no eyes, anymore: a strip of embroidered cloth hid the unhealed hollows. Yet any novice who assumed she could escape notice for some indiscretion would soon feel the sting of Mother's cane.

In the darkness of the deep caves, the Hall of Scribes was lit only by a few wan oil lamps. In the centre, on a small dais, was the Bearer of the Text; a nun chosen by the Mother for this honour. She was naked, trembling slightly.

Around her were seven novices; each had a steel pen. Inkpots stood on the dais; the ink was red, so dark it was almost black in the dim light.

At a signal from Mother Beatrice, they began scribing. With careful calligraphy, they each transcribed the pages of the document which they had been given to remember. Tiny letters on the skin of the Bearer.

The hall was silent, apart from the rat scratching of pens, the clink of ink bottles, the Bearer's whimpers, and the slow tapping of Mother Beatrice's cane.

Chapter Three: First Scars.

Hours rolled by; the work got slower, as the novices had to take turns to hold the bearer upright. Her feet needed to be lifted, one at a time, to have text inscribed. Her breasts held so that the undersides were accessible.

Finally, they were finished, and Mother Beatrice scrutinised the Bearer, before finally nodding. She selected two novices to support the Bearer; they were nervous but obeyed, of course.

Mother Beatrice carried the lantern in one hand, as they descended the ancient spiral staircase. The steps were wide and time-worn, bowed with the passing of feet.

At the bottom, the Mother leads them out into a huge cavern, and to the edge of a subterranean lake. The water looked black; its surface only visible when it caught a stray glint of pale light. On a look from the Mother, the novices lowered the Bearer, bowed rapidly, and hurried back towards the staircase.

"Kneel before our God, Bearer," said Mother Beatrice, using her cane to manoeuvre the Bearer into a position of rough obeisance.

The Bearer was unable to stop herself shivering, but tried to obey.

Nothing happened for five minutes, ten minutes. Then faint ripples on the dark water.

And then their God burst forth. Its terrible beauty would drive most insane. Scales and spines, claws and rasps, tentacles and hungry mouths. There was a truncated scream from the Bearer as the God enwrapped her in its abhorrent tentacles. She disappeared into the unholy mass of the God.

Soon the surface on the lake was still again.

Mother Beatrice waited, in the roaring silence of the cavern. Finally, a few ripples on the lake's dark surface, and a voice. A voice that had been old when this cave had formed, and old when the first primitive proto-humans had knelt before it. A voice full of malignancy and decay. The voice of God.

"Excellent," it said.

Barbs pushed past me and pressed the send button.

"Bed," she said, with a glint in her eye. I obeyed, of course.

***

That afternoon we went to the park. Barbs has this thing for nature; maybe it's because she works with computers all day. Or was that trite to suggest? If she hated nature, I'd have given the same reason. My brain was stuck in novel mode; forgetting that people could just like stuff. Or could they? Maybe they had just forgotten the reason.

"What are you thinking about?" asked Barbs.

The wilder parts of the park—the bits that Barb prefers—were still pretty park-like. Or at least the paths were; neatly edged, with plenty of signs telling people not to walk on the bluebells. It was too early in the year for bluebells now, but Barbs kept us off their areas. Apparently, compressing the topsoil over them is a bad

Chapter Three: First Scars.

thing. Honestly, I think the bluebells are overly delicate if they can't deal with a couple of gay girls walking over where they were going to be.

"Wondering why you love nature," I said. "You know, working it out through psychology and stuff."

"I have actually told you," said Barbs.

"Have you?" I said.

She sighed. "I just do."

The wooded part of the park had several small lakes. Barbs led us to one of the first places she had found; a tiny hillock overlooking a pool, hidden from the path by a copse of spindly trees. It looked harder to reach than it actually was, and once there, you could sit on a fallen tree and survey the water.

Unlike Barbs, I don't really see the point. To be clear, I am pro-park and pro-nature, it just doesn't do much for me personally. A pretty scene, sure, but thirty seconds is enough to take it in. Obviously, I don't say; I am a good girlfriend.

"Don't worry, Pearl," said Barbs, with a sigh. "We'll get moving soon." She took a packet of Tuc cheese sandwich biscuits out of her pocket. She took one, and passed the pack to me.

She munched in near silence for a while. "I suppose, when I was little, the outdoors was an allowable escape," she said. "I mean, it was male coded, I guess. People didn't have too much trouble with me splashing through streams and collecting conkers."

"I'm sorry, did you grow up in the 1950's?" I asked.

43

"Oh shush," Barbs said. "I grew up in the shadow of the Wrekin. My parents probably thought I was torturing squirrels and/or huffing aerosols, but those are male coded too, so it was still better than playing with my sister's dolls."

Barbs looked at the pool for a while; its surface was a dull silver, like ancient armour.

"What I really got out of it was," continued Barbs, "here was a world where my sex didn't matter. Where I could put aside that stress and pain for a while. The rabbits didn't care that I wished I was a girl, the kestrel neither. They don't give a shit."

"Yeah," I said. "I hate when birds are transphobes."

Barbs chuckled. "So, I guess that's why I like places like this. The human world is such shit, sometimes. People, family, society, they seem so full of malice; especially for people like us. Nature is an escape."

"You've told me this before?" I asked. I did sort of remember.

"Yes," she said, through a mouthful of biscuit. "Don't worry; I know you don't listen. You're a writer; the words only flow outwards."

"I'm sorry," I said. "I'm a crap girlfriend."

"Nah," she said. "You're pretty good." She leaned across and kissed my cheek, leaving biscuit crumbs. It was very quick; we were both nervous about public displays of affection, but there was no-one around. (On an evening walk, we had once almost tripped over a couple fucking behind a bush. We were all terribly British and made our

Chapter Three: First Scars.

apologies. Barbs wanted to warn them about compressing the topsoil, but I managed to persuade her not to. It left me wondering whether our aversion to outdoor PDA was somewhat over the top. But then I'd remembered that we would be doubly hated if we revealed that we were both transgender and had an actual sexuality.)

"Now," said Barbs, "why won't you let me read your book?"

This was going to be a problem; I hadn't told her about Paul, or about Peter and Robb. I hadn't lied to her, exactly, but I knew she was expecting a tale of trans lesbians, written by a trans lesbian. She would be upset when she realised it was not transbians all the way down. I would see how Beatrice reacted, first of all. Maybe the market had changed, and she'd want me to rewrite it with lesbians. I mean, unlikely, sure, but it would make things easier. Less likely to be read though.

"It's not really your kind of thing," I said. "I don't think you'll like it. Perhaps when I've gotten more feedback."

Barbs made an 'uff,' noise. "Why don't you think I'll like it?"

"Well, it's not like my other stuff, Barbs," I said. "You know, my short stories are mostly sci-fi and/or erotica. My first book was sort of queer litfic, but full of lead weights, I'm guessing from its reception."

"And this one?"

"Crimance, I suppose," I said, cringing as I said it. "Romance and crime."

"I like romance and crime," Barbs said. "Those are, like, transgender fundamentals."

"More of a thriller, really."

"I like being thrilled!"

"Maybe later," I said. "I'm shy about it."

Barbs looked at me for a moment. "Okay, babe. When you're ready, of course."

I was aware that this was not actually solving the problem; indeed, it was probably making it worse. This has always been my attitude to problems. It's not a good attitude. But what was my alternative? Being honest?

Barbs put the half-eaten packet of biscuits back in her jacket, and we walked on.

***

That evening my phone chimed; I hoped it was Beatrice responding, but no, it was just my mom calling ahead to check I was in, and also to give us ten minutes to prepare. These minutes were hard won; she had walked in on Pippin and someone's dad getting 'rather handsy' with each other, and reluctantly decided that she should check whether I was home before visiting.

We quickly tidied up the kitchen and living room.

Marcia unlocked the door; she wouldn't consider knocking while she had a key. It just didn't compute for her; she had a key so she should no more knock than I would. She did own the place, after all.

"Hi mum," I said, hugging her.

Chapter Three: First Scars.

"Hello Pearl, hello Barbara and Pippin." My mother never used my deadname, even in the early days, but she weighted the names in an odd way, like she was still consciously remembering to use them.

She put the kettle on, and immediately started getting the mugs out.

"I can do that, Ms Campbell," said Pippin.

"Nonsense, nonsense," said my mother. "Two sugars, isn't it, Pippin? And none for you, Barbara?"

Barbs nodded; she was not on speaking terms with her own parents, and was very suspicious as a result. If mum detected this, she gave no indication.

She talked with Pippin and Barbs about their work. These meetings always had this staid, uncomfortable quality. My mother was always polite, and never deadnamed or misgendered; I was aware that many trans folk would kill for such a mother. It was all artificial though. Or, not quite artificial, but sort of staged. She was playing the 'cool mom who is at peace with her child's transition'. She was doing that because she loved me. I tried not to forget that, but I wished she was more honest.

"And how are you, Pearl, dear," my mother asked.

"Fine, fine," I said. "Er, is there any particular reason you're round, mum?"

I noticed Pippin slip away.

"Can't I visit my daughter?" she asked, but in a rather pro forma way.

Mum was high up in the legal department of an NHS trust. She had a law degree and was 'active' (whatever that

A Rotten Girl

meant) in local politics. She had once shaken hands with Keir Starmer.

"It's very nice to have you here, Marcia," said Barbs.

"Thank you, Barbara," Mum said. "At least *you* are nice and polite."

"No, it's just—" I began, shooting an evil look toward Barbs.

"I've been talking to Trevor," my mother interrupted. Trevor was my dad. "Pearl, please consider unblocking him."

"Why do you still talk to him?" I said. "You must remember how shitty he is?" They had divorced when I was in my early teens.

"Whatever disagreements we had, or still have," said my mum, "our lives are still partially entwined; emotionally if not legally. We have a daughter, Pearl."

"Oh, is that what he says?" I said. Barbs touched my arm; she could feel the bitterness in my voice.

"Remember, Pearl, it's all rather new to your father. He thought you were just experimenting with nonconformity," said Mum. "He's not used to you being a girl. It's harder for a father."

Marcia glanced at Barbs, looking for support. "You must have seen the same with your dad, Barbara?"

"He certainly hit harder, if that's what you mean, Marcia." She moved her hand to indicate the scar at her hairline. Her voice was cold now; she got like this when defending someone. Defending herself; she simply didn't bother.

Chapter Three: First Scars.

The mother paused; her script disrupted. Finally, "I'm sorry, Barbara."

Barbs shrugged.

"But Trevor isn't like that," my mother said. "He knows he's said some things he shouldn't have, and he's sorry."

"Okay," I said.

"He wants a relationship with you."

"I said okay. I'll unblock him." I said. I squeezed Barbs' hand.

"Thank you, Pearl," said my mother. "Now, why don't I buy us all a takeaway? Pizza or Chinese? See what Pippin wants."

My phone chimed. It was from Beatrice: "Wonderful."

*
**

Lord Peter was limping. It had been a tough trail, away from tracks, sticking to the woods. Everything was a trip hazard; bracken on top of networked branches, over mud, or gaps where the rain had washed a small channel away. Robb was impressed that Peter was still going, despite his delicateness. Robb was in his element; it reminded him of military exercises. He was uncomfortable and tired, sure, and the bullet graze on his arm stung, but this was nothing he wasn't used to.

Peter was struggling, Robb thought, but quite heroically.

A Rotten Girl

"Let's stop here," Robb said.

"I can keep going," said Peter, gritting his teeth.

"No," said Robb. "We'll hit roads soon. Our enemies have trucks. Best we tackle that in daylight, when they have to watch out for civilians."

Peter nodded in the half-light, looking a bit lost.

"Sit here," said Robb, pointing to the lee of a fallen oak. "I'm going to build a bivvy, er, a bivouac, a shelter."

It was very rough; a few sturdy branches covered in bracken, more bracken on the ground. Robb could build better, but he'd have to turn his flashlight on. And a neat shelter might catch the eyes of their enemies.

They had no choice but to sit close within the shelter. Peter shivered.

"No fire, I'm afraid," said Robb. "Too easy to spot."

"Right," said Peter.

Robb hesitated, and then put his arm around Peter. Lord Peter went still, and then relaxed into it.

"You like the outdoors, don't you?" said Peter. "Hiking, building 'bivvies', and all that."

"Well, I would prefer not to be hunted across it," said Robb. "But, yeah. Life is complicated. People are full of malice. Nature is simple; often harsh, but not malicious."

Peter said, "I cannot stand it. My father made me go grouse shooting once; I hated the noise, the killing, the mud. I just wanted to be back in the library. My father is an

Chapter Three: First Scars.

excellent shot, but I was evidently embarrassing enough that he didn't ask me again." Peter rubbed his hands together.

"Are your hands cold?" Robb said, and took them in his own hands. Lord Peter's hands looked tiny and pale, compared to Robb's beefy and weather-worn paws. Robb gently rubbed some life back into them.

"How did you get that scar," said Peter, touching a raised mark on the web between Robb's thumb and forefinger. "If you don't mind me asking."

Robb shrugged. "Dunno. Probably a knife fight in Morocco, or maybe opening a tin of beans. I have too many scars to remember where I got them all. Except the first, I suppose."

"The first?" said Peter. Robb guided his hand up to another raised mark at his hairline.

"I didn't get on with my dad either," said Robb, quietly.

They sat in silence for a few minutes. Then Peter angled his head, and kissed Robb, delicately on the corner of his mouth.

A pause, and then Robb kissed back; roughly, full on the mouth. Peter whimpered, and surrendered to it; blushing as their lips mashed together. They shifted, so that Robb's body pressed Peter's down, still kissing. They could feel each other's hardness through multiple layers of clothes.

Outside the shelter, the woodland dripped with the remnants of the earlier downpour. Somewhere, a nightingale trilled.

Chapter Four: Don't Tell.

Paul is much better at being edited than me. I resent it. For *Transient Tattoo* I made the suggested changes; reducing the rambling, trying to stay in one tense, actually deciding between American and British styles, etc. I was clenching my jaw all the way through; did my editor have no artistry, no sense of poetry? I composed emails in which I impressed even my editor with my passionate defence of my words. I didn't send them, naturally, and the edits improved the book considerably. Not enough to stop it flopping, of course.

But Paul, maybe through the virtue of not existing, is a lot chiller about everything. My editor wants 'torch' replaced with 'flashlight' so the yanks don't think that Robb is assassinating his way through Minecraft; fine. I suppose that makes sense. At one remove, all the suggestions make more sense; they aren't daggers aimed at my heart. It probably helps that Lisa, my editor, loves the manuscript. She is professional; this is a job to her, but underneath that there is genuine regard, affection even, for the text. Obviously, it's not the first time anyone has liked my words, even if you exclude friends and lovers, but she dealt with this stuff for a living and still liked my writing. Or liked Paul's writing, I suppose.

Anyway, I'm getting ahead of myself. Beatrice began submitting the *Muzzle and Escutcheon* manuscript to various publishers in the right markets. At this point, Beatrice was already calling me Paul. I don't know if she had fully forgotten about Pearl, or just considered it an awkward subject, but she gave no sign I had ever been anyone different.

When *Transient Tattoo* was out to various publishers like this, Beatrice had nearly declared it 'dead on subs'. (Which might be an okay name for a BDSM murder story). But finally a small publisher picked it up. Well, beyond small, really. A micro publisher that mostly did poetry and some gay litfic, and was going broke. It's like that old joke; it's easy to make a small fortune in publishing—just start with a large fortune. Well, this publisher—let's call them White Star Publishing—decided that trans litfic was going to be the next big thing. How much crack was smoked to arrive at this decision I do not know. They didn't seem to have any particular liking for the manuscript; it was just their hail mary. I thought my editor was probably transphobic, although that might have been because he kept correcting my grammar.

This time it couldn't have been more different; several small-but-not-that-small publishers were interested. There are basically four grades of publisher; ones everyone has heard of, ones readers have heard of, ones authors have heard of, and ones no-one has heard of.

Chapter Four: Don't Tell.

I was getting interest from grade three publishers, upper grade three. Might not sound amazing but compared to grade four, it was incredible. Beatrice hinted that I should be careful not to be taken in by their admiration; they knew authors were generally desperate and praise-starved dogs. She told me to look at the numbers instead. I split the difference; Westwind Discus didn't have quite the best numbers, but they coupled that with genuine enthusiasm. Well, it seemed genuine to me; I haven't had much experience with enthusiasm. Westward Discus had a gay romance imprint called Apollo Flings; they usually called it AF. This lent discussions a surreal air, with "Welcome to AF" being misinterpreted by my brain, even though "Welcome to as fuck" didn't make any sense.

This all took ages, by the way. Months. The fucking Queen died in the middle of it, though for unrelated reasons, I assume.

One problem was my voice. Obviously, I stuck to email and WhatsApp as much as possible, but they wanted at least one phone call. Luckily, I'd been very lazy with my voice training, plus I had boy-voiced to my dad for an age, so I got through it. I was worried the whole call that I would out myself by slipping into my normal voice. I was also worried that my muddy gender-slurry attempt at a voice was maybe too camp; I was supposed to be a professional, not a drag artiste. But they seemed to find Paul passable, even clever, so I put down the phone happy, and then had the weirdest dysphoria spiral ever.

I was lucky, again, with the contracts; I hadn't gotten around to legally changing my name, so the paperwork had a male name. Not Paul's name, obviously, but my deadname. I just told everyone I went by Paul now. If you are cis, they just let you do that; it's only if you're trans they behave like you're scamming them by trying to avoid your 'real' name.

In her WhatsApp messages, Lisa, my new editor, remarked on how witty she found me. Like most people with issues around self-esteem, it was difficult to not immediately fall in love with her. The only thing that stopped me is that she was obviously straight; not even mostly straight until several cocktails in, but absolutely millimetre-precise straight. She had a long-term boyfriend, Roman, who she seemed mostly exasperated with, but affectionately, like a pet. I understand this is normal for heteros. (Trans girls would never participate in puppy play.)

So Lisa loved the book. Enthused over the characters and their romance. I was pleased; Lisa was exactly Paul's targeted demographic. We—Paul and I—had taken aim with our sniper rifle and headshotted the fuck out of Lisa.

She made a particularly big deal about Paul being a gay guy. Oh, she didn't put it like that, of course, but pointed out that, for some reason, most of the writers in this space were women. She didn't say heterosexual women, and definitely not cis heterosexual women, but I knew the truth. I pretended to be startled by her revelations.

Chapter Four: Don't Tell.

"It might also surprise you to learn that a lot of the AF imprint has a sizable female readership," Lisa confided over WhatsApp.

"Oh, really?" Paul replied. "That's great! But why?"

"I guess that women like me are interested in, you know, equality and things like that," said Lisa. "But also in, like, lived experience. Which is where you will offer something quite new."

"I'm not actually an assassin or a noble."

Lisa typed several cry-laughing emojis. "LOL. But your lived experience went into the stories, right? Particularly the relationship between Peter and Robb. I sensed a lot of authenticity there."

"You got me," I said.

"So, you're Peter, right?" said Lisa. "And is Robb based on someone real?"

"Yes," I (Peter/Paul/Pearl) answered. "Kinda. A mixture of a few men. Past lovers." This was a lie; Robb was just imagination and Barbs.

"Brilliant," Lisa said. "And that really comes through in the manuscript. Your readers are going to love it, I can just tell."

And, as I say, Paul responded well to the editing. There were a couple of places where there was, not disagreement exactly, but mild confusion. For example, I had a couple of references to Robb's body hair; I pictured him as sort of midway between a twunk and an otter. (Pippin and I had this big chat about which side—gays or lesbians—had the stupidest names for types. Gays won.) A

A Rotten Girl

twunk is a hunky twink; an otter is a sleeker and more muscled bear. Robb was big, handsome, physically fit and quite hairy.

"You're the author, of course, but maybe think about removing the references to body hair?" typed Lisa. "Our audience, they generally prefer smoothness."

"Really? A lot of my gay friends," I said without thinking, "and me, of course, like a bit of body hair."

"Oh sure. Some women too," said Lisa. "What I'm suggesting is just don't mention it either way. Let the audience decide."

"It's just, Robb's no nonsense; I don't see him waxing, or doing electrolysis, or using Veet or going for laser," I said.

"Well, it's sort of don't ask, don't tell," said Lisa. "You don't have to spell out Robb's personal grooming routine."

"Hmm." I didn't know why I was objecting so much. I hated my body hair only slightly more than I hated getting rid of it. "Okay, I'll rework it. The happy trail reference in chapter five might take a bit of rewriting."

"Brilliant!"

The other thing was Zdenka. She was a fairly minor character; my ersatz 'Q' and reluctant compadre. Oh, that's Q in the Bond sense, not the maga conspiracy or John Sherwood de Lancie. She was a technician who worked for Robb's employers. A cold type, at least at first, who is always very short with Robb. She was—ah, I'll show you.

Chapter Four: Don't Tell.

Zdenka's desk was neatly organised; electronics, scopes, tools, keyboards, laid out as if in a museum.

"Z, can you access manufacturers' databases?" Robb asked, without preamble.

"I prefer to be called Ms Kolesárová," Zdenka said, without looking up. "As you well know, Mr Casement." She was a tall woman, a bit on the plain side. She wore a roll neck jumper over black slacks and sneakers.

"You know that name's fake," Robb said.

"And you assume Zdenka Kolesárová isn't?" said Zdenka. "What do you want, Mr Casement? I have work to do."

Robb plonked the dirty boot on the table, splattering bits of dried mud onto the ordered surface. "I took this off one of our assailants. She got into a bit of difficulty and had to leave it behind. It is without branding, labels or maker's marks. Quality military boots, women's sizing, unbranded, for corporate or security use. Can't be too many manufacturers; can you get me a list?"

Zdenka sighed. "Possibly. Has the boss signed off on this?"

"Not yet," said Robb. "I need it to be quiet as well."

Zdenka shook her head. "I can't—"

"Z, please," interrupted Robb. "I really don't want to blackmail you."

She laughed. "What do you think you have on me, Mr Casement?"

Robb leaned closer. "Zdenka wasn't the name you were born with, but it is your real name. The ring you usually leave in your car has 'Lily heart emoji Zdenka' inscribed on the inside."

"How—"

"Occasionally, you forget and place it in your desk drawer instead," said Robb.

"Yes, I'm a lesbian, Mr Casement," said Zdenka. "That was never illegal, unlike your sexuality. This office is quite old-fashioned, but I assure you that we will both be injured by such a revelation."

Robb sighed. "I really didn't want to do this," he said. "But I could tell the old-fashioned office about why you wear polo necks or scarves all the time."

She looked angry. "The boss knows."

"Of course," Robb said. "The effect is very good, expensive; part of Mr Herald's offer? I expect you could bare your neck now without attracting attention; I'd be very surprised if a tracheal shave wasn't part of your surgical makeover. But I guess that old habits die hard. It's a real shame that this office is so old-fashioned."

Zdenka balled her hands into fists. "Very well."

"I might be out of line here," said Lisa. "But what's the intention of this scene?"

"To show how clever and ruthless Robb is," I explained, "especially in defence of Peter. He's a

Chapter Four: Don't Tell.

contractor, a hired killer. He gets more sympathetic later on, but at this stage he's a bastard."

"This character, the woman, Z," said Lisa. "She's a trans gender?"

"Yes."

"Mmm, she is a bit unfriendly," said Lisa. "Wouldn't it be better to have her as outright evil? Perhaps an enemy spy? I mean, what a disguise, if you think about it?"

"I think that would be unfair to trans folks," I said. "I have trans friends." This last was a cishet cheat code, explaining why anyone should care about us. A real person knows us.

"Oh, our audience is very tolerant of trans genders, of course," said Lisa. "I just worry this is confusing for them. They don't really like politics."

"Her existing isn't really politics," I said.

"No, no, I'm sure you're right," said Lisa. "But how would you feel about another *don't tell?* Sometimes what you don't write is as important as what you do."

"Fine," I said. Paul was fine with it. I would have to be; it wasn't as if one textual trans character made much difference.

"Brilliant. You are such a joy to work with," said Lisa. "Perhaps Z and Robb should flirt a bit?"

"A gay and a lesbian?"

"Just friendly flirting," said Lisa. "Might appeal to our audience. Just an idea; you're the author, after all. But it will give them someone to identify with."

Hmm.

Probably the most troublesome thing was quite late in the day, when AF asked me for an author's photograph.

Paul did not have a photo, because he did not exist. I had photos, of course, but even if I went maximum boymode, I wouldn't fool people. Well, not everyone. And I'd dropped hints about Paul's appearance; hints that I clearly didn't match.

"I'll see what I can do," I typed back. Then I panicked as I tried to think of a solution. They probably wouldn't accept a picrew.

I tried those 'the face does not exist' sites; the faces I generated were frightening and nothing like Paul. They are also supremely un-author's-photo-like. Author's photos are meant to convey something, by means of subtle background clues; authoritative (leather-bound books), nerdy (comic books), studious (normal books), adventuresome (swords), idiotic (Roman statuary), down-to-earth (a field), tough (a mountain), racist (a jungle), or female (ornaments). Okay, I decided that working out authorial photograph signifiers was not the best use of my time.

I decided that the best use of my time was making a cup of tea. Pippin was watching *Naked Attraction* with some dad (Mike? Will? We had been introduced, but they weren't at the friends-remember-your-name stage of dating yet.)

Pippin was a sort of visual model for Paul, I recall. Could I take a photo of him? He would never see it published; that would mean looking at a book, after all.

Chapter Four: Don't Tell.

But even Pippin would think it suspicious if I sat him in front of a bookshelf and told him to look intelligent and amusing. And then tried to photograph him, secretly.

I remembered that Pippin, like me, maintains a Facebook profile. For me, it's mostly to stay connected to family members; I can easily be safe-for-work because I don't care about it. None of my family has my Twitter profile; even mum (who mostly retweets Labour). Pippin also doesn't bother with other social media. I couldn't say for sure, but I'm suspicious that this is because a lot of his targeted dating demographic regard Facebook as *the* social media. Along with two-year-old memes, Pippin also posts a lot of selfies.

Leaving my cup of tea unmade, I rushed back to my room, and began scrolling through his photos. For once I was glad rather than jealous of how photogenic he was. While I would take dozens of selfies from increasingly obscure, even arcane, angles until I got one that didn't make me shudderingly dysphoric, Pippin (like Barbs) clearly had a deal with the God of Selfies (Narcissus, I guess). Even in his wasted sofa shots, he looked cool and stylish. There is nothing like spending half an hour looking at a handsome twink to make you reconsider not being bisexual.

Eventually, I found a suitable picture; a three-quarters view of Pippin gazing off to the side, mostly blank kitchen wall behind. I saved it.

A Rotten Girl

I googled 'gun blueprint posters'; well, I needed some sort of signifier. There were plenty, as Americans exist. I right-clicked.

Please don't tell anyone, but I have a pirated version of Photoshop that is almost old enough to drink. I fired it up. I placed the gun poster on our kitchen wall, using the perspective tool until it looked right; I had to mask Pippin's shoulder so that it looked like the poster was behind him. I cropped the photo, lowered the saturation, made the shadows more prominent, and messed with filters until deep into the night.

Finally, I had an author's picture worthy of Paul. He was gazing off into the distance, contemplatively; surrounded by shadow, an FN SCAR-H diagram barely visible behind him. Ideally, I'd have got some gay romance in there too, but they don't do blueprint posters for cock rings.

I sent it off. I knew that this was a bit of an unusual way of creating your author's photo, but everyone edits and filters nowadays.

"Excellent!" AF said.

***

Paul was certainly having an easier time of it than Pearl. An easier time with photos, in fact.

One day, Barbs arrived home and immediately went in for a hug. Her eyes were wet, not quite crying, but close. This wasn't the first time I'd seen her near tears, of course.

Chapter Four: Don't Tell.

She was butch, but she was also a trans girl. Still, it was unusual for her. I never knew what to do in these situations; I just held her, which always seems a bit of a nothing action. My mum deployed hugs like this, always with the appearance of counting under her breath.

"Sorry," Barbs said. She always apologised for getting upset. "Just me being daft."

"What's happened?"

"Nothing, nothing," she said. She hugged some more. "Do you ever think I should be more femme?"

"What!?" In the transbian femme community the general attitude towards butches was the same as a dragon's attitude to gold. True, there were a tiny group of femme-for-femme idiots, dragons sleeping on a hoard of cream cakes or whatever, but they were rare and shunned. And a domme top butch like Barbs? That was like winning the lottery.

"I'm, like, fairly masc," she said. "But I really don't want to be a man, or even look like one."

"Of course not!" A cleverer person than me could probably explain why the 'masculine' style of butches (if you even want to call it that) was different to the masculinity of men. Maybe we made a mistake in calling it 'masc'; men definitely cannot approach the zenith of butchness. Not even close.

"I posted a pic from the station; I thought it was a nice pic," said Barbs.

"It was," I said. I had liked and commented. Not exactly a thirst trap, but at least a little dry-mouthed; a few buttons of her shirt undone, half in shadow, exuding butch cool.

"Then a chaser liked it," she said. The term chaser covers a range of creatures, from the 'worship trans and put them on a pedestal' sorts to the 'aha, marginalised people, yum, daddy likey.' To be honest, we mostly tolerate the first set; it's unhealthy for all of us, but we don't get a lot of worship.

"A man?" I guessed.

"Yes," Barbs said. "And worse; a gay man. At least a straight guy would have been thinking I looked woman enough for his stupid fetish. But no, I am a bloke. Assigned Male At Chaser."

"No, Barbs, no." I was cold. I wanted to check my phone, but that would obviously be insensitive. "He's clearly an idiot."

"He commented, 'Looking cool and sexy, babes'," said Barbs. Shit. That was Paul. Me. I'd been doing some promo work on his Twitter; I'm not stupid enough to follow Barbs, of course, but I sometimes search her profile just to, you know, gaze at her or whatever. And I must have forgotten I was logged in as Paul.

Obviously, this was the moment to confess. We'd probably laugh about it. My sweetie was upset and... I know, alright! I know.

"Let me make you a cup of tea, babes," I said. "Sit on the sofa, I'll bring it through. I might liberate a couple of Pippin's Hobnobs too."

Chapter Four: Don't Tell.

I quickly opened Twitter while the kettle was boiling. The post was gone; she must have deleted it, taking my stupid comment into the ether with it. Probably for the best; why don't we all pretend it never happened? Why upset her more by revealing the truth?

※

Zdenka's desk was neatly organised; electronics, scopes, tools, keyboards, laid out as if in a museum.

"Z, can you access manufacturers' databases?" Robb asked, without preamble.

"No 'Good morning, Miss Kolesárová'?" Zdenka said, without looking up. "No 'I bought you a fancy coffee, Miss Kolesárová'?" She was pretty, about average height, nicely dressed.

"Sorry Z, I'm in a rush," Robb said.

"Fine, since it's you," said Zdenka. "What do you want?"

Robb cleared a space on the desk, and set the dirty boot down. "I took this off one of our assailants. She got into a bit of difficulty and had to leave it behind. It is without branding, labels or maker's marks. Quality military boots, women's sizing, unbranded, for corporate or military use. Can't be too many manufacturers; can you get me a list?"

Zdenka nodded. "Sure! Has the boss signed off on this?"

"Not yet," said Robb. "Can you keep it quiet?"

She laughed. "I won't tell if you don't, but this had better be worth the largest, most expensive coffee. With all the toppings."

Robb leaned closer. "You've got it, Miss Kolesárová."

Chapter Five: Cover Reveal.

I don't get a say in the cover, of course, but they did send me a draft copy. I gazed at the paperback for a while; a 'Not for Sale' ribbon was emblazoned across its front. It was a fairly standard M/M cover; assembled from photographs bodged together. Robb is centre stage, naturally, bare-chested and gleaming. So much for leaving body hair up to the reader. He holds an MP-5 in one hand; well, I'm pretty sure it's photoshopped in. The model is kind of giving the camera a look of confusion. Which, to be fair, I would also look confused if I was topless in a forest with a gun glued to my hand. The front of his boxers had a little union jack decal, as if it was sewn into the band. I was grateful that, at least, they haven't done the full flag underwear. It's how you know it's a serious novel; the international hitman only has a small national flag on his undies. Peter is also on the cover, but in an offset, misty section. Presumably this is like picture-in-picture, or maybe Robb's thoughts, but it looked a little like a strange portal in the woods. Peter sat on a throne, for some reason, under a massive shield.

Paul just said, "Cool." At least I wasn't paying for it.

My audience loved it though. I had spent a lot of time building a carefully curated following. The bulk were fujoshi, naturally, then reviewers of M/M books, some M/M authors, and a smattering of straight transfem authors. My editor, of course, and the AF account. Oh, and The-Hated-Authortrix, because she is funny. She soft-blocked me instantly, though. Bloody homophobe!

So I/Paul got ready for the book launch. ARC readers enjoyed it. It was actually getting a bit of a buzz. By which I mean, people other than me were discussing it. Seriously, that took some getting used to.

My only problem was that I couldn't share my excitement with Barbs. Not only was there too much history to explain to her, she would also probably remember Paul as a creepy comment guy. Plus his picture; that was another thing I had to keep hidden from her. She would get weird about it, and probably tell Pippin.

So I contained my excitement as the early reviews came in. I told her my book had died on subs, but I was researching a new one. I don't like to lie, and I don't pride myself on such things, but I'm pretty good at running a deception.

*
* *

"Tell me what's going on," said Barbs, in the half-light. We lay in bed, spoonwise; Barbs was the big spoon.

"What?" I said.

"If you've met someone else, you can tell me," Barbs said. "You were the one who insisted on exclusivity, remember?"

Chapter Five: Cover Reveal.

I breathed out.

"Unless you want to split up," she said. "That would be very sad... but—"

"No, no, nothing like that," I said quickly. Barbs voice takes on this odd, deadened tone when she's sad. She says she goes emotionally numb when upset. I suppose she has her upbringing to thank for that. Emotions are a luxury.

"I've seen you smiling at Twitter and grinning at WhatsApp. That's not normal," said Barbs.

"It's just..." I panicked. I wanted to tell her about my book. I was proud of it. But it was Paul's book. "I'm just finding my writer friends to be very uplifting at the moment?"

"Writers, uplifting!?"

"Well, perhaps uplifting was the wrong word," I said. "Maybe I mean witty. Funny? That sort of thing."

"Hmm," said Barbs. "Still doesn't sound right. Give me an example."

"Um, no, it's all writerly stuff, jokes about participles, and the like," I said, trying to hide my desperation. "You wouldn't understand. Writer humour."

"Hey, coding is sort of like writing!" protested Barbs.

"No."

"Yes," Barbs said. "The point of writing is to convey information, emotions, and/or meaning to the reader, right?"

"Well, that's simplifying it, but sort of, yes." It was actually annoyingly accurate.

A Rotten Girl

"Well, coding is about conveying meaning to one particular reader, the computer, using a simple language."

"You can't think, 'Shall I compare thee to a summer's day,' is anything like, 'one plus one equals two!'" I said, shuffling back against her.

"Firstly, you don't need to tell a computer that one plus one equals two. Somebody has already told it that," said Barbs. "And second, Shakespeare was saying, 'My BF is better than an English summer,' right? Well, computers don't care about that, but if you want, you know, to pay an extra bonus to employees who meet certain conditions, then I can write a quick sonnet to do that."

"It's not the same thing," I said, rubbing myself against her.

"No, not the same," said Barbs, "but it is writing, and to a much more demanding thing... audience," Barbs trailed off. "What are you doing?"

"Nothing," I lied. I could feel her erection pressing into me.

"Well, if you keep up that nothing," said Barbs. "I'm going to have to rail the fuck out of you."

"Please," I whispered.

"I'll fetch a towel," said Barbs.

* * *

Gay sex—gay sex between men, that is—is terrible. Oh, I'm not being homophobic. Gay guys seem to like it; fair

Chapter Five: Cover Reveal.

enough. But to a lesbian, the idea that men have a sexuality seems like a major mistake. It doesn't seem like a real thing; lesbian sex is subtle, passionate, hungry. Non-lesbian sex is like a pantomime version; jerk and release, and a quick joke. Obviously, sex between men is not as bad as straight hetero sex; at least gay sex usually has a measure of mutual respect.

Now, I know what you're thinking; is there really that much difference between two cis gay guys and two trans lesbians, who haven't had 'the surgery' yet, in terms of having sex. Same posts, same holes, right?

Well, no. For a start, they smell better than gay guys. Also, if they're on hormones, the transbians' dicks might well be slacking off. But the big difference is... hard to explain.

The easy version is: they're women.

The harder version is, well, it's mostly internal. Hell, say you're talking about two trans women not yet or only just on hormones; physically, you probably can't tell. But it feels very different. I liked women before I knew I was trans, and I liked women afterwards. In the same way, even. But sex transformed from something I was bad at, which left me embarrassed and ashamed, to something that was actually fun. Being trans is full of that sort of thing; changes behind the scenes of life. Like boymode is more an attitude than a wardrobe; you can watch a trans girl slip in and out, depending on whether she trusts the people she meets.

All that is to apologise for making the gay sex in M&E reskinned lesbian sex. Luckily, I don't think anybody can tell.

Mostly the sex is actually between Barbs and me. Barbs and Robb are dominant tops. Peter and I are pillow princesses. Well, whatever the male version of that is; pillow prince sounds wrong. Anyway, Barbs is by far the best sexual partner I've had, so I've tried to reflect that in the writing.

The first time I kissed her, back here, on her first London trip, was amazing. We were in the living room, taking turns to infodump. She was talking about... something; I don't remember what. I was watching her lips move; pressing and parting, a dart of tongue while she was thinking, a little shine. I tried to get myself under control; I wanted to kiss her so badly.

She stopped mid-sentence and looked up. "Can I kiss you?" she asked.

I fumbled for a reply. I slid closer to her and finally managed to say, "Yes."

She moved in toward me slowly, tilting her face. She paused with a couple of inches of air between us, and brushed my cheek with her hand. She was warm. We breathed the same air for long moments; it was rich with her scent, cedarwood and moss.

"Look at me," she whispered. My gaze was fluttering everywhere, but at this instruction I met her eyes. They were dark, and sad, and I felt such open-hearted love for

Chapter Five: Cover Reveal.

her that I was taken aback. She moved her hand to my chin, and closed the gap. I shut my eyes.

The first kiss was very soft; a gentle meeting of skin on skin. I shivered slightly; my mind quieted, focusing on that fleeting contact. She kissed me again; lips meeting for longer, pressing into one another. I murmured, though I wasn't trying to say anything. Then we mashed and gaped our mouths together, pulling apart with saliva trails, then back together. Her tongue flitted in. I surrendered my mouth to her, jaw softening. Other parts were not softening.

So kissing, frotting, oral, anal; it's all secretly she/hers. If I thought my book was going to be read by gay men, I'd feel bad, but luckily its audience are straight women. I suppose that makes sense; if your type was straight men, then you've obviously got to look elsewhere for enjoyable erotica.

***

So, yeah, pre-launch went well; but I was anxious about the launch. PTSD. True, TT had never received any buzz, but the ARC readers had liked it. It was only on launch that its utter failure had become obvious. A bottle of champagne cracking against the hull, a controlled slide down the slipway, and then straight into an iceberg parked outside the dock.

I had to watch a good book sink without trace; of course I was afraid for the not-good book.

A Rotten Girl

"Don't worry, Paul," said Lisa. "Pre-orders are looking great! I know you're concerned about people being homophobic, but that's just a few religious nuts. Over here, at least. Obviously, foreign countries are still a bit behind..."

She was a good editor, but I wouldn't trust her judgement on gay rights.

But she was right about *Muzzle and Escutcheon*.

Oh, I don't mean that it took the publishing world by storm; it wasn't outselling *The Bible* or the latest Dan Brown. But nobody cancelled their pre-orders, and sales got off to a good start.

I had several 'interviews' with gay romance 'magazines', i.e. answered emails from blogs. They seemed to go well; Paul was humble and erudite, with an occasional edge of humour. I mean, he was like me, but as a man he got a pass on being annoying.

Early readers produced their reviews, with the upshot that it was well worth the purchase, "... for fans of spicy encounters." Oh, the reviews were not unreserved in their praise: a lot of reviewers had a problem with the name. I had misjudged how familiar the word 'escutcheon' was to normal people; I blamed my youth of reading Arthurian stories and playing D&D. I knew what a 'Bohemian earspoon' was, for example, and that it had nothing to do with Queen, ears, or cutlery. A few people also objected to 'muzzle' as there was no BDSM-style muzzling going on. I should have just called the thing *Gun and Shield* and had done with it.

Chapter Five: Cover Reveal.

Others thought that the crime/assassination plot distracted from the romance. Excuse me for wanting a framework to hang their relationship on; it was hardly overly gritty, it had bloody 'knockout gas' for fuck's sake. A few said it was 'political' which I can only assume was because the nobles are depicted as wanting to retain their power. It was hardly advocating for regicide. But I forgot that there is a sizable contingent of people that believe that nobility is a solemn burden shouldered reluctantly to save us regular folk from the dreadful horror of being rich and powerful.

And yes, these criticisms stung, but they're a whole lot easier to take when they are a couple of lines in an otherwise glowing review.

It even did well on booktok; Robb and Peter's relationship was subtle and nuanced, apparently. I was less pleased with this comment once I worked out that it was just because it wasn't obviously pure grumpy/sunshine or enemies to lovers. Of course it was rich/poor and forbidden love, but they barely noticed that. A bit of average writing could serve as a cloaking device for these well-worn tropes.

"Paul, the book is a success," said Beatrice. "A genuine success." If Beatrice was saying it, I could allow myself to believe it.

"It fits the market so well," Beatrice continued. "It has the gay sex that they want, enough crime to say it's serious and edgy."

A Rotten Girl

It didn't really have edge; it just had enough weight to the plot that people could pretend they weren't here for the sex. Not that there was anything wrong with that; I had written erotica before. Just I'd written lesbians for lesbians, not gays for straights.

Anyway, Paul's follower count skyrocketed. Other M/M authors—women, of course—began to tentatively include me in their discussions and jokes. They were cis, so the jokes weren't all that funny.

My book was a success. People were reading and enjoying it. I was being acknowledged as a proper author. Well, Paul was.

I had to be careful not to give anything away to Barbs, after that last confusion. I was still sad about that. Luckily she was in Wrexham for most of the week. It was a bit of a monkey's paw thing; she was the person that I most wanted to share this with. The one woman who was only supportive of my authorial ambitions. And the one who would be most annoyed about the lying.

I told mum about it, kind of; I knew she wouldn't ask about any details, like the title, but I could at least explain that it was selling well, and get a parental pat on the head.

I told dad as well. "Is it in Waterstones?" he asked.

"It's online only, Trevor," I said.

"Just on those kibbles?"

"Well, you can buy it for your e-reader, or in paperback."

"You want to get it in Waterstones. Ask your publishers," he said.

Chapter Five: Cover Reveal.

"I don't think that's practical."

"Get it in the window," he continued. "You'll get foot traffic that way."

"Again, I don't think that's practical."

"Tell your publishers," he insisted. "You don't get anywhere without asking. Do you think John Grisham is afraid to ask his publishers about window displays? No."

"Fine," I lied.

"Or get some paperbacks, and sneak them into the shop. People will buy them."

"They won't be on Waterstones' system!"

"They are a business, they won't turn paying customers away."

"Well, even if that was true," I said, "which it isn't, I wouldn't see any of that money. I would be subsidising Waterstones."

"You've got to speculate to accumulate," said dad. "They will want to get in on the action. You need to have more faith in your book."

"I'll bear that in mind."

Even when dad was supportive, his phone calls made me feel worse.

Pippin was nice, though supremely uninterested. Like, I saw someone once who made and played stone-age lithophones; "weird but cool," was my reaction. Pippin reacted the same way to news of the 'book'. But he promised to get his friends to read it. Which, I realised with horror, I didn't actually want, since Paul's back cover photo looked a lot like Pippin. Because it was Pippin.

"Muzzle and... Escalator, right?" Pippin asked.

"Um, Muscle and Escalator," I said. "Because of the weight training and... running up escalators?"

"Oh cool," said Pippin. "Great title."

He high-fived me. Crisis averted.

***

Back on Paul's twitter, women were posting M&E excerpts. Mostly scenes before the sex scenes; they didn't want to out themselves as pervs, I guessed. It worried me at first; that it would turn into mockery. I spotted several awkward turns of phrase; it was written with a degree of contempt for the genre after all. I don't think I've done any male equivalents of breasted boobily but who knows. (He *cocked dickerly to the stairs, and penised upwards?*)

But no, they liked it; praising the 'spice'. They—fujos—couldn't say it made them horny, so they had to do an amateur dramatic rendition of *Dune*.

Spice was sex divorced from all the messy realities. Sex without visiting the bathroom first. Sex that didn't need towels. But it brought in new readers, so I used the chilli pepper emoji liberally in Paul's responses.

***

"And then there was Lady Cecelia," said Lord Peter. The safehouse was a little run down; the supplies were up to date, and it was clean, but it hadn't been lived in for a while. "She's several cousins, and one bastard, away from the—"

Chapter Five: Cover Reveal.

"May I kiss you?" asked Robb, interrupting. They had kissed before, but that had been almost accidental; comfort taken a step too far. This, thought Robb, was deliberate.

Peter froze. His porcelain throat moved as he swallowed. Then a tiny, "Yes."

Robb moved his face toward Peter's. He went slowly, as if stalking a timid animal. Robb paused with still a couple of inches of air between them. He brushed Peter's cheek with his hand. Robb's fingers were warm and calloused; strong but gentle. The two of them breathed the same air for long moments; it was rich with their scents. They had used the same inexpensive shower gel, but under that was Peter's faint smell of bergamot, and Robb's cedarwood.

"Look at me," Robb whispered. Peter's blue eyes were downcast, but he raised them at Robb's instruction.

The first kiss was very soft; a gentle meeting of skin on skin. Peter shivered slightly. Robb kissed him again; lips meeting for longer, pressing into one another. Peter murmured; mouthing nothings into the warm air. They mashed their lips together, pulling apart with saliva trails, then quickly back together again. Robb's tongue pressed insistently into Peter's mouth. Lord Peter surrendered his mouth to Robb. Peter blushed; the mutual stiffness was obvious to both of them.

***

A Rotten Girl

"Um, Pearl, could you check on your girlfriend?" asked Pippin.

"Hmm?"

"She's still in the loo," said Pippin. "And I really need to go."

Barbs had gotten back almost an hour ago. Her trains had all been late, her phone battery was dying, and she had been, "Desperate for a shit."

I had been cooking a rather involved mushroom curry, attending to Paul's tweets while I waited for onions to caramelise. I stirred them again.

"I'll text her," I said. I heard her phone warble from the living room.

"It's charging," said Pippin.

"Oh right, yes."

I made my way to the bathroom, down a useless bit of corridor mainly used to make sure the flat didn't break planning permission.

"Um, sweetie, are you okay?" I said, softly rapping the door. "It's just that—"

"Out soon," Barbs said, monotone.

I backed off. When Barbs emerged, she was carrying a paperback. Familiar. A 'Not for Sale' ribbon across its terrible cover. Muzzle and Escutcheon.

Chapter Six: Being Noticed.

In writing, dialogue is never real. People don't speak in sentences. Most of the time they mess up the grammar. Half of what they say is 'er' and 'um'. So why don't authors—realistic authors—write it like that? Because it's terrible to read, and—perversely—seems a lot less realistic than fictional dialogue. Less detailed, but also focused on the important things we wanted to tell the reader. In fiction, Barbs would have been definite that we were breaking up.

She packed a large bag. She never really moved in, but her stuff had gradually accumulated.

"I'll stay on the sofa tonight," Barbs said. "Get going tomorrow morning." Her voice was monotone. She was too sensible to be a trans girl wandering about the capital, looking for a place to sleep.

"Let me explain," I said.

"Explain what?" she said. "You are Paul Sisters?"

"Yes," I said. "But it's just a pen-name. Lots of people have pen-names. Women especially."

"Pearl, I don't care about the name," she said. "Galbraith it up for all I care. I just wanted to confirm no-one was spying on us."

"What do you mean?"

"It has a lot of us in it," said Barbs. "Memories that I thought were precious. No, that were precious, at least to me. Turned into scenes for your stupid book."

"It's not stupid."

"Our first meeting, our first kiss, our lovemaking. I thought that was important."

"It was," I said. "All writers are inspired by life, Barbs."

"I'm not sleeping with all writers," she said. "I don't want to be grist for your mill."

"It's not like that," I said. I was starting to cry. Barbs might have been, too.

"No, it's worse," she said. "Robb is based on me, right?"

I nodded. "He's very cool. Like you, he—"

"I don't care," Barbs said. "He's a man. You know how much I have overcome not to be seen as a man. How insecure I am that fools will mistake being butch with manliness. My womanhood was hard won, so I don't care if man-me is a fucking ninja. I don't want to be a man."

"I know," I said. "I'm not a lord either! I needed men for the book."

"Why would anyone need men for anything?"

"I'm writing to the market, Barbs," I said. "Straight women love this kind of thing."

"Well, they can write it then."

"They do," I said. "But I think I can do a better job."

"I'm sure, but why the hell would you want to?"

Chapter Six: Being Noticed.

"As I said: marketability." I sighed. "Beatrice was right. I got nowhere being authentic. Fujos love their men-on-men, I am going to exploit that. Am exploiting that."

"By grinding our love up, and telling them it's delicious man-pap?" she said, coldly. "Catering to those ridiculous male-worshipping she-dogs? And all for money."

"No!" I said. "Or sort of. I wanted to sell in reasonable numbers. I wanted other authors to respect me. And it's all happening. I just wanted to be read."

"You were read," said Barbs. "I read you. But I guess I misinterpreted."

***

She left in the morning. She still had a room in her cousin's place, just outside Shrewsbury.

I sat and watched telly. Pippin touched my shoulder, and washed up the pan of burnt curry without complaining.

"Come to the club with me," he said. I shook my head. "I've had a lot of break-ups," said Pippin. "Alcohol, dancing and poppers are the best cure."

"We might not have split," I said. "It might be a temporary break, a rest. She wasn't one hundred percent clear."

"I liked Barbara," said Pippin. "But lovers don't go 150 miles from you on a maybe."

I sighed. "I didn't want to ask for clarity, because I was afraid of her answer."

Pippin shook his head. "Alcohol, dancing and poppers, my friend."

I eschewed his suggestion; well, almost. I did help myself to several of Pippin's lagers, and settled in to watch a *Grand Designs* omnibus. Always a good reminder that money is in no way related to competence. Finally, I opened Paul's Twitter, and read fans squealing in pleasure. It wasn't like I didn't see where Barbs was coming from; lesbians hated being compared to men, and transbians doubly hated it. And rightly so; some (men) play up the similarity between straight men and lesbians, "We like the same stuff, after all." Well, we're not the contingent who think women are stuff.

But, for all I understood Barbs, I didn't see why she didn't just do a genderswap on it. Lesbians learn this skill early; there is so much heteronormative crap that it's a survival skill to think how easily *Romeo And Juliet* could be a lesbian drama. I mean, unnecessarily poisoning yourself: that's some lesbian shenanigans.

If Barbs had just done a mental find and replace on *Muzzle* and *Escutcheon's* pronouns she would have realised how much of a love letter to her it was. I scrolled onward in a haze of self pity.

"Er, is anyone else picking up something between Robb and Zdenka?" said a twitter message from a user called MMDrarry. There were several comments in reply: a mixture of assents and dissents. They ranged from,

Chapter Six: Being Noticed.

"Being friendly isn't flirting!" through, "It's all on Zdenka's side! But I'd do the same!" to, "Book 2: throuple?"

I had to award Lisa some points for this; she had predicted exactly how the audience would react.

Username Laios-mouthfeel at'ed me; "Paul, is Robb pansexual?" That was annoying. Non-authors often assume that characters exist outside the book in some way; to be fair, authors are often to blame for this misconception. "Sometimes a character leads you in an unexpected direction!" is almost always bullshit, and when it's not it's either self-deception or incompetence. We—authors—control the totality of the characters, and further, any 'fact' about them is only true because it exists in the story. Oh, one might have character details that haven't made it into the story, but until they've made it into print, they can change. I hadn't said whether Robb was bisexual; I had indicated that he was at least homosexual by example. I thought he was pure gay, but that was because I didn't have a plot point that required otherwise. So was he or wasn't he? Stupid question. Unknown, undecided, mu, null.

I was, however, reasonably sure that replying to a reader with, "Stupid question," was probably a no-no from a fan engagement perspective.

"Robb is as bisexual as I am," I typed. "That is to say, he isn't; but never say never."

That seemed to keep them happy enough. Well, I got a couple of frowny faces from my few gay readers, but M&E wasn't for them, despite the gay sex.

I scrolled on, occasionally dispensing authorial bon mots.

Twitter username Laios-mouthfeel posted Paul's picture with 'never say never' written across the bottom in a glittery font, as well as a couple of hearts. Ugh. I ignored it.

***

"You are lucky you are heartbroken, or I'd have totally drawn a moustache on your face," said Pippin, when I awoke. I was still on the sofa, but I could tell it was very late. My mouth felt like something had died in there, and all the moisture had been sucked into the mummified corpse.

"Oh," said Pippin. "I didn't mean to be transphobic. It's just moustaches is what they always drew. Curly ones."

I rattled an open can of lager; there was a swig left. It was extremely flat and not terribly pleasant, but it did make my mouth feel like something that might belong to a human again.

Pippin raised an eyebrow. "Wow," he said. "Tonight I've given a BJ to a guy who's not sure he's gay, in a club toilet that probably isn't hygienic, after doing a couple of

Chapter Six: Being Noticed.

bumps, and I still feel I'm doing better in the got-it-together department than you."

"Yeah," I said. "Gender swap it and clean the toilet and that sounds awesome." I stretched; hearing more cracks than I wanted to. "You didn't bring the totally-not-gay guy back then?"

"Nah," Pippin said. "As soon as he nutted, he started crying about his wife. I don't want to be unfeeling, but maybe think about how much you love her before cumming in my mouth."

"Convenient," I remarked.

"Yeah," said Pippin. "Want a cup of tea?"

I nodded. What time was it? I opened my phone.

"Why is there a picture of me?" asked Pippin, looking over my shoulder.

Twitter was still open, showing the 'never say never' picture.

***

The bullet pinged off the gravel nearby. A silenced pistol, shot at long range. The dark figure taking a chance. Robb was fairly certain their pursuer was not trying to hit Peter, just him; which was good, he supposed. Tactically, their position was poor, however. In the early morning, a thin haze of mist hung over the canal, close to the water. The canal blocked their escape in one direction. Opposite, a steep embankment would hinder them in another. Their only option was to run,

89

A Rotten Girl

which was a recipe for ploughing straight into a trap. They needed options.

An annoying rhythmic puttering could be heard ahead; a narrowboat, making its way down the canal. Holiday hire livery. Their pursuers had shown reluctance to engage with civilians; they probably had a 'no mess' clause in their contracts.

Robb picked up his jog, pulling Peter along with him. The narrowboat was going at walking pace, so catching up with it wasn't difficult. At the back of it, a man at the tiller was staring at them owlishly. They were both various degrees of bedraggled.

"Ask for a ride," Robb whispered. "Use your name."

"Um, morning!" called Peter. "Would you mind giving us a lift? I, er, am Lord Peter Ukebridge-Talbot."

Peter's accent was even more cut glass than usual. The boat slowed.

"The lordship was out on an early morning hunt," said Robb. "But we were set upon by unsavoury types."

Peter nodded. "Taking us to the next town would be very helpful," he said.

The man, who had the bearing of a geography teacher, pulled to the side. "Better come aboard, sirs," he said. "Marcia, put some more coffee on."

They climbed on board, and the narrowboat continued its journey. A long way back their pursuer still followed. And

Chapter Six: Being Noticed.

canal boats were easy to track, since they needed canals. Very little capacity to get off track.

"How fast can this thing go?" asked Robb.

"Six, maybe seven, if you are in a real hurry," said the man.

"Seven miles per hour!?"

"Theoretically," said the geography teacher.

Robb sighed. "Please put the pedal to the metal, good fellow, time is of the essence. And don't worry about me; I'll catch up."

"Catch up?" said Peter.

Robb manoeuvred along the far side of the vessel, until the bulk of the narrowboat shielded him from view, and slipped into the water. Lucky, he thought, that this was a rural canal; only moderately filthy rather than deadly.

It wasn't a pleasant journey underwater to the bank, but once there the overgrown weeds shielded him from view. The still surface of the canal gave him a good reflection of where his pursuer was, however.

It is difficult to climb out of water quickly without making a lot of noise. Their pursuer was jogging now; the crunch of the gravel giving Robb an extra tenth of a second. The pursuer turned rapidly, drawing her pistol, but Robb was already spinning, foot out, water and pondweed flying off him. He kicked the gun out of her hand; he had hoped it would land by him, but instead it plopped into the canal.

He didn't have time to worry; he blocked a flurry of blows from her. He noted several martial arts, all tuned for speed not strength; Robb was fast, but she was faster. He concentrated on blocking, hoping that she would tire herself out. Finally he threw a few punches; more to probe her defences, than to injure. She was tired, but not as tired as she was making out. A bluff, Robb thought. She hadn't kicked for a while; maybe she was hoping he had forgotten. He also saw a combat knife at her belt. A solid kick, connecting, would give her time to draw the blade. That would be bad; he moved closer to the water's edge, entering kick range apparently accidentally.

The strike was fast; a spinning side kick. If Robb had not been prepared, it would have cracked a rib, which probably would have stunned him enough for her to stab him. Instead, Robb jumped back, and as the foot went past him, he grabbed it and span. She spiralled rather than let her ankle break, but Robb's movement had brought her over the edge of the canal. Robb didn't let go of her foot. There was a lot of splashing. It is perfectly possible, thought Robb, to drown someone like this; holding them upside-down, their upper body in water. Robb wondered if he'd have to. Her other leg was kicking out; he'd have a few bruises, but she wasn't in a position to do serious damage. Her head kept dipping below the surface. She was getting weaker, or seemed to be; Robb was wary of deceptions.

Chapter Six: Being Noticed.

She jackknifed her upper body out of the water; she had the combat knife in her hand. Robb hadn't even seen her draw it, and now he had no time to react.

She brought the knife down on the laces of her boot, cutting them, and her foot slipped out. Robb almost toppled back at the sudden release. The would-be pursuer made a couple of graceful strokes, swimming to the other side of the canal. A stand-off. Robb would be foolish to enter the water, especially with his enemy having a blade. He could—theoretically—throw stones, but he had never heard of an assassin taken out like that. She could throw the knife; but it is hard enough to kill someone with a single knife throw, especially when tired and waterlogged. And if you don't kill them, you've given them a knife. Plus Robb still had hold of her empty boot; having only one boot was a serious impediment to the outdoor assassin.

Without breaking eye-contact she began to back off. Robb did the same, until there was enough distance between them that he could jog to the high-speed getaway boat.

***

"Okay," said Pippin.

"Okay?" I echo.

"You wanted to pretend you were a man, for writing. So you needed a man's picture," he said. "You should have asked first, but I'm quite proud you chose mine."

"You are?"

A Rotten Girl

"Sure!" he said. "Your author is cis?"

"Yeah."

"So I pass!"

"You know you pass," I said. I *could* pass, depending on context, and whether my observers had been primed to watch out for a tranny. But Pippin was, to even a trained observer, just a little (cis) guy, a short (cis) king.

"I still like to hear it!" said Pippin.

"Fair."

"I don't remember posing for this pic though."

"It's photoshopped, it's just a picture of you in the kitchen."

"Ah, right," said Pippin. "You can take more photos of me doing writer stuff if you want. You know; I could have a quill, or be looking at words, or something like that."

Pippin had a strange idea of what writerly activities were, but I was enormously relieved he wasn't making a fuss about the photo. If only Barbs had been so chill. I missed her, but maybe it was her fault for not being more laid back?

*
**

"So great we get the good spice," typed Laios-mouthfeel, "from an actual man. You can almost smell it!"

I was reading Twitter again.

"Are we sure?" said someone of user name Guelfan. "Us women of M/M have been caught out before."

Chapter Six: Being Noticed.

"You can call us Fujoshis," said someone with username Fujojoba. "We've reclaimed it."

"The book was definitely written by a man," said Laios-mouthfeel, annoyingly. "A gay man. He's almost as excited by the sex scenes as we are."

"Right," typed Guelfan. "That's what I'm saying; 'he' could be one of us. I don't know any guys who like gay sex."

"Do you know any f*gg*ts?" said Fujojoba. "But I see your point. His profile is a bit bare."

"Well, what were you expecting," said MMDrarry. "A sex tape?"

"That *would* prove things," said Guelfan.

"You people need to be more accepting," typed Laios-mouthfeel. "Anyhow, I can feel he's a man because his writing makes my womb twitch."

"TMI," typed Fujojoba. "But I think the rest of us just have to live with the mystery."

I quit out of Twitter, and texted Pippin. "About those author photos…"

***

"A reading?" I said, "at a convention?"

"Aphrowriting Con is a major event for readers and writers of romance," messaged Lisa. "It will boost sales."

"As I said, though," I repeated, "I'm very shy. I'm sure I'd just be a panicked ball of quivering insecurity."

A Rotten Girl

"No, no," said Lisa. "They are all very friendly. Everyone liked your new photos didn't they? Our readers love even the tiniest bit of connection with their authors."

I had taken three more photographs of Pippin. One where he was gazing meaningfully out of a window at a cloudy sky. One 'funny' one where he was reading a book, but holding it upside down in a hilarious and side-splitting visual joke. And one, at Pippin's insistence, where he's in running gear, drinking a glass of water, and his top is 'accidentally' rucked up to show a glimpse of abs and washboard tummy. Three guesses as to which one got more likes.

"Well, I'll have a think about it," I said. "Talk to my friend."

"Why don't you invite your friend?" said Lisa. I was fairly sure she thought that by 'friend' I meant 'lover'. "We'll have a Windward Discus intern there, but I know having someone familiar can help when you're shy."

I had a stupid idea. Pippin didn't read, but he *could* read. Would it be possible to train him to read out a section of M&E? Maybe give him a few plausible answers, and be there to feed him any more involved responses? That would be stupid, right?

"Maybe."

"Don't take too long; slots go fast," said Lisa. "Hotel rooms too."

Why did I even entertain the idea? I think I've become a bit too used to the praise. It used to be just Barbs and a few other trans girls who would say nice things about my

Chapter Six: Being Noticed.

work, but now they were loads of cis girls. Their praise is effusive too. Is it really so wrong to want to bathe in that admiration, to drink deep from the well of devotion? I was trans; the only thing we are normally praised for is shutting up. I had gone so long without acclamation that I had no immune system against it.

"Is it somewhere exotic?" asked Pippin.

"Not unless you're one of the few people who thinks Birmingham is exotic," I said. "But we wouldn't get much of a chance to see its wonderful vistas, anyway."

"It does sound quite cool though," said Pippin. "I'd be like a spy, undercover, pretending to be an author, but really being a normal person!"

"You'd have to take it seriously," I warned. "This is my reputation that's on the line."

"No problem!" Pippin said. "Pippin Peterson, superspy, double-oh eight!"

"Paul Sisters," I said, "author."

"Right, right."

Okay. Praise ahoy, then.

**

Once I asked Barbs why she hated being praised. Oh, I pretended to hate it, but inside I was purring like a catgirl. She, however, really hated it, to the extent that it affected her mood.

"Just, you know," she said, stroking my hair, "that whole mortifying ordeal of being known thing."

Marcia and her then boyfriend Greg had invited us to spend a couple of days on their holiday barge. I was not a fan. The British countryside is already boring, it is not improved by scrolling past torturously slowly. But Barb liked it and would sit up the front, just watching the dull nature inch past. I sat with, or lay with her, for as long as I could bear it.

"Yeah, but it's more than that, isn't it?" I said. I was lying on the cushions, my head in her lap. It felt safe enough to do that; in the rural countryside, people who walk down towpaths are either visitors (who are more interested in herons or carp) or locals (who will consider anything—from owning an electric scooter to being transgender—as undifferentiated city nonsense). The most physically dangerous sorts—groups of tanked-up lads—are fairly rare here, and the canal is wide enough that Greg could put six feet of water between us and any transphobes.

"Camouflage is about not being noticed," Barbs said. "That was my escape, when I was young. Stillness. It's why I love nature; if you stay still, the natural world opens itself to you. I've had foxes trot past; they know I'm there, they can smell me, but I'm not moving, not dangerous. I have been surrounded by a herd of deer. I was leaning against a tree and they just didn't see me. They scattered when I changed position though. So I guess I thought that safety was not being observed. And people have to notice you to praise you."

Chapter Six: Being Noticed.

"It was just winning at Trivial Pursuits," I said. "They weren't trying to give you a Nobel prize. Or burn you for witchcraft."

"Maybe," she said. "Although Greg was a bit disgruntled. He hid it well."

"Yeah, well, geography teacher, I suppose," I said.

"Yeah," said Barbs, twiddling my hair. "Ooh, kingfisher!"

She pointed it out. It was like a normal bird, but shiny. Pokémon-ass thing. But Barbs loved it.

Now I'm crying again.

Chapter Seven: Consonance, Perhaps.

Forced Proximity and Only One Bed; it felt like an odd case of real life being slightly tropey. I think sometimes there are two types of writer; those that deliberately use tropes, and those that accidentally use tropes. Oh, most of us writers think that we don't use tropes; that just puts us in the second category.

Pippin and I shared a hotel room. I vowed to stick to him like glue for this conference; I didn't want him to be caught out with any writerly questions. Although there were Actually Two Beds; I wasn't sleeping with Pippin, although we have gotten somewhat closer over the preceding weeks.

Of course, I'm very anxious during check-in and sign-up. "Whose idea was this?" I kept saying to Pippin. He drove us up in his little Kia; it was sunny, and Pippin had Taylor Swift on. The dreadful British countryside even went by at a decent clip, since traffic was mostly okay. And I was just worrying, and missing Barbs. Though she would probably hate this.

Anyway, we got name badges; I was jealous of Pippin's "Paul Sisters" badge. Which is a fucked up thing for a trans girl to think.

A Rotten Girl

Pippin's big challenge was tomorrow; he would read a section of *Muzzle and Escutcheon*. He didn't appear nervous; I was. The rehearsals had gone fine; Pippin was an excellent speaker, and—perhaps more importantly—confident and an extrovert. If he tripped over a word, he would simply correct himself and continue. If I tripped over a word, I'd probably have a panic attack, and then confess the entire scheme, and possibly the JFK assassination.

The next morning, Pippin turned and said, "Do I pass?"

He was wearing just underpants; I had seen him before in similar states of undress, going to or from the shower, but it was still a bit of a surprise.

"Well, I think you ought to wear more."

His chest had the marks from his top surgery. Technically scars, but faded and benign looking. Like broad smiles.

"Pearl," he said, exasperated, pointing down.

The shadow of something deformed his undies. A big dick, it looks like.

"What's that?" I said.

"New packer," he said. "I think Paul is hung, right?"

"I don't actually know."

"I do," he said. "All authors have big dicks. Writing is pulling it out and slapping it down."

"I think literature experts probably have a different definition," I said. "But thanks for making me dysphoric about my chosen profession."

Chapter Seven: Consonance, Perhaps.

"Okay, okay," said Pippin. "Authors are big dicks *or* massive cunts, is that better?"

The convention itself was in a different set of buildings, but the same complex. There were some confusing corridors to reach there, or a walk outside, around a fountain.

I was becoming aware of the sheer size of the convention, and more importantly, how many people there were attending. As a trans girl, I have an entirely reasonable reaction to crowds. Outright fear. At any moment, I thought, they could go zombie mode. Or terf mode, which is exactly the same, but smells very fractionally nicer. My 'cloaking device' (passing) was holding up, at least for now. The place had lots of readers and writers, so people had to accept a wider range of normal than they were used to. Pippin, of course, was unfazed by all of this; his major problem was that most of the limited number of males here were his type.

Oh, there were some gay guys here for the proper gay romances, and a few fey boyfriends here to be good pups, but what really seemed to catch his attention was the number of dads reluctantly accompanying teen daughters or middle-aged wives.

"If you think about it," Pippin whispered, "they are evidently not prudish enough to stop their wives or daughters from reading romance, so..."

"So they are probably not prudish enough to turn down gay sex?" I said. "Look, own-voices and everything,

103

but that seems to fundamentally misunderstand both prudishness and gayness."

"I'm just saying," said Pippin. "They look pretty bored…"

"No relieving them," I told him. "You've got a job to do, remember."

"I'm thinking about various jobs," Pippin said. "But okay, Miss Section 28, I hear and obey."

The convention itself surprised me; I was expecting a romance convention to be all pink and hearts, like a valentine's card that had escaped into reality. But while there was a bit of that, on flyers and signage, there were also a lot of rural or comfy cottage signs, and a lot of 'seductive' signage (which is mostly crumpled linen and the author's name in flowing script). Oh, there were rainbows too, as a sort of semiotic prefix. Het rural romance was a thatched cottage; gay rural romance was a thatched cottage with a rainbow. The Windward Discus stall had a seductive style sign, with the names of the various imprints and a tasteful rainbow circle in one corner.

Windward Discus actually had two people there; the intern Xan ("Short for Alexander, yeah?") and BSC Ruth ("Lisa mentioned you."). No, I never found out what BSC meant; I presume she wasn't just telling us she had a Bachelor of Science degree.

This was the first in-person test of my deception. Obviously, I let Pippin introduce himself first; he remembered his false name, no problem, and introduced

Chapter Seven: Consonance, Perhaps.

me as "my good friend, Pearl." Fortunately, they were only interested in ticking off paperwork; I was pretty much ignored. Which made me both glad and slightly annoyed. We chatted for long enough to count as polite and then checked out the rest of the conference.

The organisers had split the books up into three sections, presumably because they had three main exhibition spaces. Spice, No Spice/Closed Door and Young Adult; the Spice one theoretically had a minimum age, although the harried woman doing the enforcing was mostly answering queries and giving directions. Windward Discus's stall was in Spice, in the M/M region. Actually, most of the LGBTQ+ books were in here; I got the impression that a same sex kiss was automatically spicier than a het kiss.

We watched another reading; to make sure that we knew the sort of thing to expect.

"It would be just our luck if there's a 'Now relate your plot through interpretive dance' section that Lisa forgot to tell us about," I said.

"I'm a good dancer," said Pippin.

"Okay, crisis averted."

The reading was from [a moderately successful writer of M/F contemporary romances]; even though you're in my head it feels like it would be rude to say her name. Also, authors can be a bit litigious, and I'm not ruling out the existence of psychic lawyers. Look, her work isn't for me, but heteros must enjoy it. A village veterinarian on night shift falls in love with a village baker, on early morning bread shift. It is every bit as good as my summary suggests.

She read it well, however, even though Pippin and I had to suppress giggles at the first meeting with the baddie; a local government officer who wanted to knock down both the vet's surgery and the bread shop in order to build council houses. "Critical support to Mr Raze," I whispered.

She took the normal Q&A, nothing unexpected there; mostly standard Qs, apart from questions about the minutiae of previous books.

"Oh, you're so lucky to have your boyfriend accompanying you to these," said a woman on our way out of the room. "My husband wouldn't leave the bar."

"Oh, we're just friends," I said.

She leant closer. "You might think that, but he might think differently."

I didn't say that Pippin would be more interested in her husband. Or that, as non-heterosexuals we sometimes actually communicate about relationships.

"I do think differently," said Pippin. "I think we're best friends." He said it in what you might call the gay accent.

She looked suspiciously at us both, and hurried onwards.

*
**

Once again, Robb took Peter's hand, helping him to his feet.

Chapter Seven: Consonance, Perhaps.

"We've got to get away from here," Robb said, illuminated by the light of the burning Rolls Royce.

"The police—"

"Can't be trusted," said Robb. "If they can get to your father's driver, they can get to anyone."

Peter sobbed. "Poor Wentworth."

"We have to move," said Robb, pulling Peter behind him. He led him down dark side streets until the sound of sirens was lost behind them.

"We need to get off the streets," he said, as they walked toward a plain hotel. "Ever stayed at a Principal Tavern?"

"What do you think?" said Peter, tiredly. "They haven't even got a doorman."

"I'll book us in," said Robb. "I'm going to say it's mister and missus, just in case anyone is keeping an eye on registrations for two men. So... um, try and walk like a woman."

"This is the Lytleigh Boy's dramatic society all over again," said Peter. "It was a rugby school; very few slender boys. I had to play Juliet, Ophelia, and the like."

"Shakespeare? We didn't do him," said Robb. "But, prithee keep your head down."

The room was small and mostly clean. Mostly; not enough that anyone would complain, anyway. Robb checked for bugs, though if anyone was smart enough to plant them here, in a random room in a random hotel, Robb would know they had bigger problems. Nothing. Peter also checked the

A Rotten Girl

room; examining the trouser press like it was some alien artifact.

Both were trying to ignore the one bed, but eventually Peter sat down on it.

"Right, we should sleep," said Robb. "Tomorrow we need to get out of the city. Visit Zdenka. I'll take the chair."

"Robb," said Peter, very softly. "I'd very much prefer it if you didn't." He unbuttoned his shirt.

Robb paused. Peter gulped. Then, with panther-like speed, Robb headed for the bed.

"What should I take then?"

* * *

We'd been given a fairly smallish room for our reading, but I was surprised and pleased to see that it was pretty much full. In fact, seeing a large group of cis girls made me somewhat dysphoric, as well as anxious. I was scared of cruel girls, but also desperately wanted to be part of that group.

Pippin, thankfully, was unaffected by girls; as a gay man he pretty much expected admiration from them.

A member of the convention staff did the introduction. He looked very bored.

Pippin's reading went well; people enjoyed the bit where they sheltered in an ersatz Premier Inn. We had practised it a lot, and Pippin was likeable enough that any mild slips were eminently forgivable.

Chapter Seven: Consonance, Perhaps.

They even laughed at the right bits; I found myself wishing I'd written it better. This was my audience after all; maybe I'd been underestimating them. It was difficult hearing Pippin get applause for my work, while I sat off to the side, like an assistant. I shouldn't resent Pippin for it, of course; this was my idea.

My next worry was the Q&A. I'd gone for the minimum time for this, but he'd have to field a few questions. Hopefully, he could remember the canned responses.

"Where do you get your ideas from?" The first question was such a cliche that we had almost decided it was unnecessary to rehearse an answer. Luckily, I have a low opinion of these people's originality. *Ah, who can say where the muse comes from*, we had rehearsed, *I'm just rather glad she does! Or maybe he does; I think my muse is masculine.*

"Who can say where my muse comes from?" Pippin said. "I'm just very glad she does! Or maybe it should be 'he does'; my muse is masculine, I think."

"Are the characters based on real people?" Okay, another one we had rehearsed; I would tear up, but Pippin could answer without any problem. *Of course, but it's never in a 1-to-1 way. Robb's love of nature comes from one person, his manner of speaking from another. I, like all authors, are rather magpie-like with other people's traits!*

"Are any of the events influenced by things that have happened in your life?" Ha, *my life as an international assassin, you mean?* Pause for laughter. *But no, mostly not for the adventure parts; I'm no Bear Grylls. I'm no kind of bear.* Pause for laughter. *As far as the spicy parts go; they tend to be based on real life, but exaggerated just a little. You know, how men do.* We'd probably rehearsed this one too much; Pippin was a bit wooden.

"What about a sequel?" *I can't say too much about that, but I am in talks with my publisher.*

"I enjoyed it a lot. Is this really your first novel?" Shit. We haven't rehearsed this. Just say *yes*, Pippin.

"No," said Pippin, glancing at me. "There was another one, about a tattoo or something."

"But that was under a pseudonym," I called out. "And it wasn't very good."

There was an uneasy quiet from the crowd, as they tried to work out what was going on. Why was his assistant speaking up, and why was she insulting him?

"I mean, that's what you said," I continued. "You regard this as your real debut novel, remember."

"Right, right," said Pippin. "This is my real debut! That other one was terrible."

"I'm afraid that's all we have time for," said the staff member. "Signing in ten minutes." Thankfully everyone applauded again, but I got a couple of dirty looks.

*
* *

Chapter Seven: Consonance, Perhaps.

I was in a bit of a spiral for the signing. Pippin had nearly given everything away. Whose stupid idea was this bloody thing?

I checked my phone, while Pippin signed copies of M&E. We had developed a simple P-squiggle autograph that Pippin could do easily and robotically. I was on guard for any questions, but people mostly stuck to compliments.

Looking online, there were several positive comments about the Q&A and one worrying one. A user, Guelfan again, said, "Went to Paul Sister's q and a. The publisher's handler didn't want him speaking about some other book. Interesting." And emoji eyes.

That was annoying, but I suppose it could be worse.

I tried to relax, but listening to Pippin get compliments that were intended for me just made me irritated.

"And can you put the message 'never say never' in there, please?" I looked up; it was the same girl who had asked the 'first novel' question.

"Ah, right," said Pippin, writing. "Robb is a bit of a James Bond character, isn't he?"

"Um, plus your twitter," I said, hurriedly. "Remember, when you were asked if Robb was pansexual? Or you?"

Pippin's face displayed a moment of distaste, but he masked it quickly. "Right, right," he said. "Never rule anything out, I guess."

111

A Rotten Girl

"Can you put a heart, too?" asked the girl. She was pretty, a bit short, and nicely rounded. As the woman-appreciator of the two of us, I was jealous of her barking up the wrong tree.

"Sure," said Pippin, glancing at me.

"Maybe I'll see you later on," the girl said. "There's usually a party."

"That sounds nice," said Pippin, either oblivious or pretending to be. He signed the book, and the girl reluctantly moved on.

***

So our primary mission objectives were complete. Not flawless, but survivable. We fell back to the Windward Discus stall and helped them sell books. Including mine, which was pretty neat.

There was a nice camaraderie among the sellers. We watched the table of a F/F Romantasy author when she went to the loo. She was having a bad day of it. Either lesbians didn't go to conventions at all, or they didn't go to this one. We chatted to a tiny press operation that did M/F romance, usually paranormal or supernatural. It was run by a husband and wife team. They both seemed boring to me. They had a Tibetan singing bowl which they rang, er, rimmed, every time they made a sale. I have long since given up trying to understand heteros.

At the end of the day, we made our way down to the bar. It was packed.

Chapter Seven: Consonance, Perhaps.

"Just a couple of drinks," I warned Pippin. "Then we go back to our room. I don't trust you not to spill the beans when you're blotto."

"Spill what beans?" asked the annoying question girl, appearing behind us with a level of stealth that would have impressed Robb.

"Er, what the sequel is about," I said.

She looked at Pippin. "Yes," he said. "Precisely."

"Well, I won't eavesdrop," she said, heading for the bar.

"Bloody hell," I said. "I don't know how spies manage it. I'm going to brave the loo; can I trust you to maintain operational security?"

"Roger, roger, over and out."

***

In the end I didn't brave the public loo; it looked crowded, and I was concerned about being clocked. I walked back to our hotel room, and had a quick shit in peace, or at least as close to peace as I could get with Pippin unattended.

When I came back, Pippin hurried across the crowded room to meet me. I had a bad feeling about this.

"Pearl, can I borrow our room for maybe a half-hour?" said Pippin.

"Why?" I probably scowled here, if I'm honest.

"I've been talking to Simon," Pippin said. "And we want some private time, if you know what I mean."

A Rotten Girl

"Who the fuck is Simon!?" Believe me, if putting an extra exclamation mark on the end of that sentence was allowable, I'd have done so!

"Simon, of Dalby Press, you spoke to him."

The husband and wife paranormal romance publishing team. I tried to picture Simon; tall, salt and pepper hair, crystal pendant, kind of fit, but with a bit of a belly. Fuck, the crystal had thrown me; he was a dad.

"That's not a good idea," I whispered. "You're pretending to be cis, remember?"

"I'll continue pretending."

"No offence, but he is going to notice," I said. "You pass very well, but that's while wearing clothes."

"I'm just going to blow him," Pippin said. "I won't be getting naked."

"Okay, but your cover..."

"Pearl, we're not lesbians," he said. "There will be no long conversations about literature while we're supposed to be making out."

I sighed. Men. "Okay, I guess. Be careful."

I was lucky to find a space at a table, and sat down to read my phone. I scrolled Twitter, as me, in this case. Barbs (we were still mutuals) had posted a picture of some brambles, under which she said was a badger; I trusted her, although the tiny piece of black and white could easily be litter. It made me smile to think of her, though; surrounded by nature.

"You lost the author?" said the question girl, sitting opposite me.

Chapter Seven: Consonance, Perhaps.

"Huh? Oh, he's doing... stuff."

"I had hoped I'd be the first stuff he'd do," she said. "But he seems very serious about this gay thing. I'm Janine, by the way."

"Pearl," I said, sighing.

"Paul and Pearl!" she said. "That kind of... rhymes? Well, not rhymes but..."

"Consonance, perhaps," I said, a bit worried. I didn't like her picking up on the similarity.

"Maybe," said Janine. "So, are you sleeping with him?"

"We are both serious about our respective gayness," I said, sighing again. "He likes men, I like women. We're friends."

"More than friends though," she said. "You're his assistant, aren't you?"

"Informally."

"You keep him on track," she said. "I noticed."

"Well, writers, you know?" See that? The cunning way I reinforced the deception, by an offhand comment.

"Yes," she said. "I've known a few. Not very practical." She smiled. "But you're like me; prosaic, down to earth, but passionate."

Was she hitting on me?

"Did you like *Muzzle and Escutcheon*?" I said, changing the subject.

"Yes, I liked it a lot," she said. "Though it was quite overwritten. I guess Paul thinks a little too much of himself. Writers, eh?"

115

I drink some of my watery coke, and sort of vaguely nod, though I'm rather insulted. But she leans forward, giving me a view of her cleavage.

"You're not like that," she said. "You try to hide away all the time. Timid. Like a girl-Peter."

"I suppose," I said. I thought I'd been insanely outgoing today!

"This place is a bit full," she said. "My room is quieter."

I nodded again. That made sense.

She sighed. "Would you like to see it?"

Oh.

"I'm transgender," I blurted out. Like, I didn't want to spring it on her, but I had forgotten about any subtlety. Although, I suppose, if she was going to reject me violently, in public was probably safest.

"I thought you might be," she said. "I really like your voice. And I'm probably pansexual. Come on, then."

Chapter Eight: Conventional Romance.

I've never been one for romances. Reluctantly, I've come to realise that this is because I'm no good at them. Oh, I did alright in the T4T crowd, where romantic incompetence is virtually a selling point for bottoms. But there's still romance; a crush, a kiss, a fumble. I fucked up the most important relationship in my life; I really should be steering clear.

Janine's room was coincidentally on the same floor as Pippin's and mine. Same inoffensive but out-of-date decor. It was single occupancy, though, and kind of smelled of girl. It smelled nice, though.

I was anxious, of course. Girl. Cis girl. Going to the room of.

But the day had gone well. The mission was a success; the stupid plan had somehow managed not to collapse into a pile of lies. Janine, if anything happened, would simply be the cherry on top.

"Sit," said Janine, gesturing to the bed. I sat. I knew how to do this for trans girls, but couldn't remember how to rizz up cis girls. It must be the same, yeah? What was the first step? Oh right, talk to them on Discord for between four and forty weeks. That might present a timing problem.

"Vodka?" said Janine. She picked up a bottle of Asda own-brand.

"Sure."

She poured a generous measure into a coffee cup. "Only one cup," she said. "I hope you don't mind if I drink from the bottle. Bit chavvy, I know."

I shook my head, and she passed me the cup. I took a gulp.

"You look nervous," she said, sitting on the bed beside me, bottle in hand.

"Yeah," I admitted. "I don't do this a lot."

"Oh, me neither," she said, taking a swig from the bottle. "Couple of conventions a year, usually. Not usually romance, even though romance is my favourite. Bad demographics, though." She laughed. "And I guess I'm trying to make my numbers up, after Covid dented them."

"With—do you mind me asking?—with authors?"

She laughed. "Mostly. But not exclusively; marketers, other fans, assistants. Conventions are like a holiday from real life, after all. And authors are the least real life of anyone. Can I kiss you?"

"Um, yes?"

The kiss was pleasant. She tasted of vodka and strawberries. It was stupid and unfair to compare her to Barbs; but Barbs' was better. But maybe that was for the best; the heady, breathless unhingement of Barbs' kisses would not help me here.

Chapter Eight: Conventional Romance.

"You kiss like an author," she said, when we broke apart.

"Er, is that good or bad?" If my deception was undone by kissing, that would be a source of both annoyance and pride.

She looked at me, as if weighing up how much honesty I could take.

"Well, from a technical point of view, not great," she said. Although this hurt, it was also affirming; this was the sort of honesty that people gave women. "You were very much in your own head, like you were narrating rather than experiencing." Okay, you'll have to imagine me giving a knowing look to the metaphorical camera at this point. "But I like that. With authors, you know that everything is being stored away. I don't want to sound conceited, but sometimes I read later scenes—sex scenes—by an author I have... done things with, and I just know that I am the bountiful serving wench or the ample cyber-whore. Do you write?"

As you probably know, under no circumstances should you offer even the subtlest chance for an author to plug her work. However, I didn't want Janine to form links between Paul Sisters and Pearl Camellia, so I hedged. "Er, I jot things down, sometimes. Not romance, just short stories; sci-fi and fantasy. Nothing published, of course."

"So you *are* a writer!" Janine said.

"Not published."

"So I'm getting in on the ground floor," Janine said. "Why don't you kiss me again?"

A Rotten Girl

This was basically therapy for my imposter syndrome, I realised. I bet Janine was popular at conventions for that reason. I kissed her; there were some tongues, some saliva. Janine was trying to kiss memorably; I was trying to remember it. It was an odd effect, but nothing to complain about.

Janine smiled, and put the bottle on the floor. I drained my coffee cup, and leaned over to place it alongside. She began unbuttoning her blouse.

"How would you describe me?" she asked.

Well, from memory; pretty, a bit short, and nicely rounded. Was that enough? Oh god, was I an author that was bad at describing women, despite being a woman? I might as well have thought, 'chubby but fit with nice bazonkas'. "Er, you're pretty," I said. I tentatively reached out and stroked her hair. Biden-ass move. "Um, a crown of golden radiance?" I said.

"Ooh, nice," she said. "What about my eyes?"

They were like muddy green. "Like a forest newly in spring leaf?"

"Mhm," she said. She took my hand and lowered it to a breast, pressing it into the fabric of her bra. "You can look, you know," she said. I flicked my eyes down, then back up to her face, then down again.

"Um, sumptuous—" I began.

"The bra is probably putting you off," she said, and shrugged out of her shirt. She reached around for the back of her bra, and removed it. I moved my hand, checking her face for confirmation, and caressed a breast. I felt a pang

Chapter Eight: Conventional Romance.

of jealousy. They were bigger than mine, and much bigger than Barbs'. So why were they so much less exciting than Barbs'? Again, they were extremely nice, fun to hold; weighty and elastic. "Generous curves of creamy softness," I said. Breasting boobily, my brain supplied. "A roseate glow," I ran my thumb around her nipple, "suffused her satiny skin." Her breath caught, and then she laughed.

"That's good," she said. "I've always enjoyed having my tits fondled. Most authors don't, you know? Fondle, I mean. Oh, their eyes go wide, like Christmas morning, looking at toys. Then roughly groping them, twisting them like dough. Trying to tune my nips into weird radio stations. [Famous author] just motorboated me, straight off." She sighed. "Why have you stopped?"

"Sorry." Because I was suddenly worried that my breast handling was wrong, or might soon be wrong. Plus a little bit of fangirling that my hands were on the same skin where [famous author] had blown raspberries. "I didn't want to, you know…"

"You're good," she said. "It's not that I don't enjoy a good groping. I quite like it rough. It's more that, oh, I don't know, it's a choice? That I should get a say. That I might get something out of it. You seem like you know I'm actually here; it's really nice, but strange."

"Let me guess, most of your authorial conquests have been men?" Nothing makes as good an argument for lesbian sex as men. "You need to sleep with more women."

"Oh right," she said. "You have tits too. Sorry, you're correct; all the authors have been men. [Famous author] was my white whale; when I finally bagged him, I thought it would be so cool. Then he motorboated, and couldn't actually get it up. Put a damper on my enjoyment of [Netflix adaptation of his work], I don't mind telling you. Can I feel your tits?"

"Er, sure," I said. "They're not very big." I pulled my t-shirt off over my head.

"They're neat," she said, fondling them through the bra. "I wish mine were smaller sometimes. Hurts my back, and a lot of bras are vicious."

"I wish mine were bigger," I said.

"Why couldn't you ask for bigger when you had the operation?" she said. "Is it an NHS thing?"

"Huh?" It took me a moment. "I haven't had a boob job, those are all hormones."

"Oh!" she said. "I didn't realise you could do that." She was gently squeezing my boobs; it was pleasurable, but not as thrilling as Barbs' hands on me.

"HRT is magic." I said. This is why I don't sleep with cis girls. Well, that and not getting any offers.

"What about... you know... your cock?"

"What about my cock?" I said. "I haven't had surgery down there either, if that's what you're asking."

"I'm sorry," she said, "this is all new to me."

I sighed. She didn't have any reason to know this stuff; I should try to be patient. They should make a "So you're about to sleep with a trans girl," training video that

Chapter Eight: Conventional Romance.

we could give to prospective cis sexual partners. Maybe with a multiple-choice test to make sure they took it all in. "Okay," I said. "No stupid questions. Go ahead."

"So your cock," she said. "Hormones didn't make it... go back in, then?"

"No, because that—" I wanted to say, isn't how anatomy works. I gathered my patience. "No. Hormones do make it work a bit differently, and I lost a bit of length. But I still have a functioning and fully external cock."

"Good," she said, and leaned in. We kissed again, and fondled each other's breasts for a while.

"I haven't been with someone with tits before," said Janine. "But I could get used to this."

"I thought you said you were bisexual?"

"They say you should say pansexual now."

"Okay, not opening that discourse," I said. "Same question though."

"Well, I said I thought I was," she said. "There are women I fancy. I like women. I'm kind of a feminist after all. I just hadn't got round to actually... Men are just easier, in that regard."

"Easy, but unfortunately men."

"So that was why I thought you would be ideal," Janine said. "Best of both worlds."

I felt shutters come down. "No," I said. "You can't say that."

"I just mean, you're halfway between the two, right?"

"Again, no." I reached for my tee-shirt. "I am fully a woman."

123

"Sure," she said. "I know that's your goal, and I'm certain you'll get there. But at the moment you've got a mixture of bits, male and female, that's all I'm saying."

"No," I said, putting my tee-shirt on. "I am a woman. My body is a woman's body. My cock is a woman's cock."

"Sorry," said Janine. "I don't understand. Women don't have cocks!"

"Some do." I stood, the feeling of ancestral transfems stirring within me. Unfortunately, my foot landed on the coffee cup, both breaking it, and pitching me forward. For a fraction of a second, it looked like I was going to land on Janine, but I managed to alter my direction even as I fell. But my knee knocked into the vodka bottle, sending it spinning, splashing floor and bed liberally with Asda own-brand vodka.

Janine swore.

"Sorry!" I said, ancestral transfems turning their back on me and sloping off. I scrambled to my feet. I picked the bottle up, and set it on its base; stared at the broken cup as if trying to remember if I had a spell equipped to fix it. "Sorry," I repeated. "I'll just go."

I bolted for the door, yanked it open, and hurried out into the hall.

I collided with a semi-dressed man, running down the corridor. For the second time in as many minutes, I went down in a tangle of limbs. This time, not all the limbs were my own.

As I and the man began untangling ourselves, I recognised him as Simon from Dalby Press. I wasn't sure

Chapter Eight: Conventional Romance.

what the appropriate greeting for this situation was. Janine appeared in the doorway, still topless, and gazed at us in shock.

And this is why it's generally a bad idea for trans people to try to sleep with cis people.

* * *

"You're speeding," said the woman. Robb adjusted the rear-view mirror so that he could see her properly. She was dressed elegantly; Robb did not know fashion, but he would guess her get-up was impressive and expensive.

"Yes, ma'am," said Robb, as they raced down the motorway. It was mostly empty, so he could put his foot down.

"Please decelerate," she said, after a few seconds. "Dealing with the police is a hassle."

"I'm afraid the speed is necessary, Miss Artemis," said Robb.

The woman looked up sharply.

"Why would that be?" she said, reaching into her handbag.

"Because I'm gambling on you not being stupid enough to shoot the driver of the vehicle you're actually in, while it's travelling at speed," Robb said.

She took her phone from her handbag.

"Jammed," said Robb. "I just want a chat."

"Well, I suppose you have gone to extraordinary lengths to arrange it," she said. "How did you know which firm I use for my cars?"

"Does it matter?" Robb said. "You will have to burn your current routines just in case."

"Unless I shoot you, and take my chance with the seatbelt," she said. "Modern cars are quite well protected."

"Sure," said Robb. "But you try not to attract notice. Oh, you'd tidy all the fuss away, if you survived, I'm sure, but it would be a note in someone's binder."

"Fine," she said. "What did you want to talk about, Mr Casement?"

"Worked out who I am, then?"

"We don't have many enemies," she said. "Not living ones anyway. But I don't understand why you are here."

"Who hired BrightTeeth?"

"Don't know," she said. "Everything was anonymised. We tried to crack it, to no avail."

"What was the mission?" Robb asked.

"Capture Lord Peter," she said. "Kill any bodyguards if necessary. No civilian deaths."

"And why did you stop?"

She looked surprised again.

"The contract was cancelled," she said. "I thought you would have known. We took quite a loss on that contract. But we failed enough times to activate the escape clause. A little

Chapter Eight: Conventional Romance.

research found that the customer had located an alternative provider. And loosened the conditions."

"Who?"

She raised an eyebrow. "That information was quite hard to find. It would be foolish to give it away."

"I can always swerve into the central reservation."

"Indeed," Miss Artemis said. "But that doesn't seem like you."

She looked out of the window; in the half-light, the countryside rushed by. Robb accelerated.

"Fine," she said. "A deal: I give you the information, and don't shoot you; you owe me a favour, and don't crash the car."

Robb gritted his teeth; he hated that price. "Fine," he snarled. "Tell me who has taken on that contract."

"The Escutcheon, Mr Casement," she said. "Your employer. That's why I thought you'd know."

"Fuck." He had left Peter with them.

"Oh dear," said Miss Artemis. "Drop me anywhere. I think you had better have a word with your bosses."

***

Pippin was in our room, face down on his bed.

"Pippin?" He was, at least, dressed.

He turned his head towards me. "I am sorry, Pearl," he said. His shoulders heaved. Crying?

No, laughing.

"What's going on?"

"I..." He gathered himself, and broke down laughing again.

I sat down, and waited.

Pippin gathered himself for the second time.

"Sorry Pearl," he said. "You're my best friend, you know?"

"Likewise," I said, impatiently.

"Okay, okay," he said. "Simon and I were making out. Heavily making out. It took a while because first he wanted us to do some ecstasy."

"Oh god," I said.

"Nah, my tolerance is quite high, and his tablets were shit. He bought them here. Can you imagine the quality of MDMA that gets sold at a romance convention?"

"No," I said. I literally couldn't.

"And then he had to spend fifteen minutes telling me that his wife was 'not very receptive to innovation in the bedroom department'. Do you think he talks like that because he's cis or because he's over forty?"

"I have no idea," I said. "I'm more interested in why he was sprinting down the corridor half-dressed."

"I'm getting there!" Pippin said. "Oh, did you see him? Obviously, I half undressed him, mainly to shut him up, but also to enjoy some delicious dad musk—"

"Please never say those words again."

"So, yeah, we're making out, and starting to get handsy," he said. He laughed again, till he was nearly crying. Then he stopped suddenly. "Where was I?"

Chapter Eight: Conventional Romance.

"Handsy."

"Right, right," he said. "So, we're both getting pretty friendly with our hands. And he reaches down my trousers, to caress my so-called dick."

"Didn't you tell him not to?"

"Well, I was concentrating elsewhere," Pippin said. "And I hadn't explicitly asked before I started playing with his... Don't give me that look, Pearl. Everything was consensual."

"Okay." I sighed. "So he discovers that you, er, aren't super well-endowed down there."

"Well, I'm wearing my packer, remember?" Pippin said. "So from his perspective, he gives me a friendly grope, as just as he's thinking 'feels a bit weird', he pulls it from my briefs. He screams, thinking he has detached my dick. He flings it and runs for the door."

"Flings it?"

"The television," said Pippin, starting to laugh again.

Perched on top of the flatscreen, between the bezel and the wall, was a limp but large dick. Well, dick substitute, but you get the idea.

"How did he manage to get it there?"

Pippin shrugged. "Maybe dicks are like cats?" he said. "Anyway, I'm sorry, but he will probably work out that I'm trans. I suppose he might just think I'm a cis man with at least one detachable penis."

"I think that's unlikely," I said, suddenly tired. "But hopefully he has other reasons to stay quiet. I'm going to fetch some snacks, and some water."

"Tuc biscuits!" said Pippin.

"If they have any, sure," I said. There was a small newsagents just outside the hotel's campus.

"You should get back with Barbs," Pippin said. "She always had good biscuits."

When I got back, Pippin was watching *Columbo*. He hadn't removed the packer, so young-ish Peter Falk was columbo-ing with a dick floating over his head.

I passed Pippin the biscuits and some water, and slumped onto my bed.

"He's sexy isn't he?" said Pippin.

"Who? Columbo?"

"Yeah."

"I mean," I said. "If I pretend he is a he/him lesbian, I suppose I can see it."

"We wouldn't have got this deception past him."

"Just one more thing, sir," I said. "I happened to notice that your john thomas detaches. Now, I asked my wife, and she says that's unusual."

***

The next morning we were both somewhat the worse for wear. Neither of us had had much alcohol (though Pippin had romance convention MDMA), so this was mainly the effect of metabolising a near fatal dose of embarrassment.

We helped with Windward Discus' stand again. Simon was missing from the Dalby Press stall, which was

Chapter Eight: Conventional Romance.

probably for the best. His wife was very standoffish; we didn't inquire.

I saw Janine in the crowd a couple of times. I wondered if I should apologise, or ask her for an apology. In the end I did nothing, apart from getting ready to hide if she got close.

It was less busy today. We went to a panel ("Writing the Sex Scene in Non-Erotic Works") more or less to see what it's like. Well, that was my reason; Pippin came along so that he didn't get into trouble. He just read his phone, and chuckled when a panellist said a rude word.

It was alright, as a panel; a lot of discussion over the 'correct' point to fade to black. I decided, based on last night, they were missing the important "transition to slapstick" option. I mean, all sex is funny; good sex is just the 'laughing *with* you' variety.

Oh, and I learned that I almost certainly use too much dialogue. "That's probably true," I whispered to Pippin.

We didn't ask any questions of the panel. It was mostly people asking questions that had already been answered, the traditional comment-disguised-as-question, and the odd question about what words to use. No, there is no more poetic word for groin.

In the afternoon, Pippin drove us home; it was threatening rain, but never actually did. We listened to the radio.

I texted Barbs, "Hope you had a good weekend!"

"I did," she sent back. Very quickly, though I tried not to read anything into that. "And you?"

I wanted to tell her everything. The whole stupid adventure. She'd laugh and console me and say something wise. If she was my girlfriend, that was. But what's the point now?

"Yes," I said.

"Cool!" she said.

I sent a heart emoji, but like in orange not red.

She sent a hug emoji.

Chapter Nine: Questionable Characters.

There is a tendency among cis liberals to go, "Cancel culture isn't real!" And they are often right; the failed academic talking in the papers about how they've been silenced, the has-been writer bemoaning the woke mob in a documentary. That's all bullshit, of course. You want to see real cancellation; try being a transfem with an opinion, a story, or, worse, a joke. A shift of opinion and a few bad-faith screenshots, and you would simply disappear. If you were lucky, a year later the cancellers would say it was an over-reaction and vow it would not happen again. Until the next time. I felt the fear, because that was the kind of silencing when you were never heard from again. Or, at least, not by the same name.

Twitter was going mad. Well, Paul's twitter. Normal Twitter was doing its normal thing; arguing about how racist it should be. I wasn't concentrating on that, however.

It had started with Guelfan mentioning, "Still thinking about Paul S's assistant glossing over a missing book."

Then Laios-mouthfeel was like, "A book the publisher doesn't want out there?!"

"Maybe because it's bad," Fujojoba responded.

"Paul is a good writer," said Laios-mouthfeel. "A touch overwritten, but we all wanted to find out how Peter and Robb managed their forbidden love." Overwritten? The bloody thing was underwritten! What sort of rubbish are they used to?

"All writers produce clunkers from time to time," said Fujojoba. "We're lucky if they only come up with a clunky title. Looking at you, M and E!"

Hmph; I didn't come to Twitter for this.

"Okay girls, I think I'm onto something." MMDrarry posted a screenshot of my 'asking my agent how hot I'm allowed to make the sex scenes,' tweet. "He's argued with his publisher before. Just guessing but what if the previous book was Just Too Hot?"

A publisher and an agent are different things, genius. And I made that up anyway.

Guelfan answered, "You may be right. Perhaps if Muzzle sells well enough, his publishers might rethink."

"Publishers do be loving money," observed Guelfan. "But maybe it's the assistant that's the problem. She said the previous book was bad."

"That's not a good thing for an assistant to say," said MMDrarry. "Jealous?"

"Thinking about it, the assistant was secretive and kind of 'off' with me," said Laios-mouthfeel. Was I? Was she even there?

"Ohh?" said MMDrarry.

The thread seemed to die there.

Chapter Nine: Questionable Characters.

A while later, Laios-mouthfeel made a new tweet, "Okay, this is #NotACallout but something happened at #Aphrowriting that I feel I should share." She had attached four screenshots of a notes app.

Firstly, I have nothing bad to say about Paul Sisters. His reading was great, the Q&A was interesting, and he was really friendly.

His assistant, however, is another matter.

They seemed nice, at first. We talked about writing. They were a bit secretive, but that's fair enough. They were obviously transexual, but I am not phobic. I am actually an LGBTQ+ myself; a pansexual, and an ally (to all, but particularly the gays).

Anyway, the bar was noisy, so we went to my room. Yes, I can sense some of you typing; don't worry, it's not that.

They change the subject to their own hobbyist writing. Now, I'm the last girl to mock someone for having half-finished drafts sitting around, but it was clear that they—the assistant—was very jealous of their employer's sudden rise in the crimance world. And of his abilities too, I guess.

But I enjoy talking to writers of any skill level, so we continued. We had a few drinks, and I suspect my tolerance is someway below theirs, for biological reasons. They mention that they are transexual, and I begin to ask questions. I apologise for being curious; I am an ally trying to learn all I could, so as to better support the T. As some of you know, I live in quite a small village, and we don't have any.

A Rotten Girl

They don't like the questions, and lose their temper very quickly and without warning. There is no actual violence, but they are taller than me. I don't normally discuss my childhood, but this brings up some traumatic stuff. They loom over me, and I am terrified. Then they kick over a water bottle, smash one of the hotel's cups, and storm out of the door.

I breathed a sigh of relief, but there was a sudden noise from the corridor. I peek out, and the assistant and someone else are brawling. I suppose it's good that they sought out someone who was the appropriate gender to fight, but I hate violence of any kind.

I was pretty upset. I wondered about giving up cons, or asking my BF to come with (but he'll get so bored).

Anyway, for a while I thought about saying nothing: but I'll feel so guilty if it happens to someone else.

For clarity: the assistant is not evil, but should work on their anger management, and be aware of the fear they can cause in vulnerable girls.

I had a panic attack. If you have ever had a panic attack, I don't need to describe it. If you have never had one, I don't think I can describe it.

Shaking, crying, vomiting, spasming. I was in my room, and just curled on the floor, even though the bed was just there. I stayed like this, in fear and panic, for hours.

I almost called Barbs. Girlfriend or not, she would have talked me down. And without judgement; Barbs had

Chapter Nine: Questionable Characters.

more trauma than me, but never lorded it around. But I couldn't call her, couldn't explain, couldn't admit. I would not be broken in front of her. I would not be a burden to her.

I remember the sensory grounding exercise she had taught me. The "five things you can see" thing, it's quite well known. It began to work.

I breathed slowly; in, hold, out. I couldn't remember how long I'm supposed to do any of the sections for, but I remembered Barbs saying *hold your breath for longer than you breathed in, breathe out for longer than you held your breath*. Part of why these things work, for me at least, is because they are a game; you focus on getting it right. The details don't really matter. You find yourself forgetting about panicking, because you have this silly exercise to complete. People are so stupid.

Eventually the panic subsided. I cleaned myself up, shakily got myself a cup of tea, and watched *Homes Under The Hammer* to further calm down.

Right, I thought, how could I defend myself? Robb mode, Barbs mode; logical, strategic. Most of what she had written was true, or true enough from her position. Nitpicking wouldn't work. And I couldn't argue with how she felt about something, either.

There were a lot of omissions though. I could point out that one of her reasons for going to conventions was to fuck authors. Of course, that was basically slut-shaming, which I didn't approve of. More to the point, it wasn't any sort of defence; unchaste women shouldn't be terrorised

A Rotten Girl

either. I could mention that she basically tried to seduce me. But that was easily twisted into "yeah, she was gagging for it," and was likely to make things worse. I could object to her they/them-ing me, but to cis people that seems like nitpicking too. I have 'special pronouns' (that is, different to the ones assigned at birth), she used special pronouns for me, so what was I moaning about?

I might as well admit it; it's hard to win any arguments as a trans girl, because so many people quietly hate you. You are the only person given less credence than a cis woman. Well, probably a POC trans girl would have it even worse, so, um, thanks whiteness, I guess.

Ugh.

The positives then: she hadn't really accused me of much, apart from anger. A lot of implications, but no concrete harm. And she was careful to keep Paul out of the line of fire. That was an advantage; she didn't know that I was Paul.

I reluctantly opened Twitter, and scrolled through the replies to Laios-mouthfeel.

"You can tell us, LM," said MMDrarry. "Was it a man or a woman?"

"She certainly seemed like a woman to me," said Guelfan. Yay, passing.

"Hmm," said MMDrarry. "But you didn't actually see anything."

"Like what?" said Guelfan.

"I think Drarry means cock," said Fujojoba. "She normally does. On account of loving cock."

Chapter Nine: Questionable Characters.

"Shut up," said MMDrarry.

"It was an author's Q and A," said Guelfan. "They didn't show cock."

"They rarely do," said Fujojoba.

"They were a trans, and I respect that," said Laios-mouthfeel. "But they were fairly keen to talk about their penis."

"Penis equals man," said MMDrarry. "And this questionable character was in a woman's room, being inappropriate. Sounds like you had a lucky escape."

"As I say, I don't think they are evil," said Laios-mouthfeel. "Just, like, a victim who blamed their allies instead of the bigots."

"Listen, this man impersonated a woman, to the degree Guelfan was fooled," said MMDrarry. "And then inveigled his way into your room."

"Oh, talking of bigots," said Fujojoba. "Enough of your man-hating, Drarry."

"I love men!" said MMDrarry. "It's just the ones that pretend to be female you have to watch out for."

This, at least, was making me angry rather than panicked. Bloody transphobes; bloody 'allies'.

My phone beeped. A WhatsApp message from Lisa. "Hi Paul. Nice sales at the weekend, but maybe a bit of trouble brewing. Have you checked Twitter?"

"Just caught up," I said.

"So, you know your friend has ruffled a few feathers."

"It's all lies and misunderstanding," I typed. "Pearl didn't do anything bad."

"Oh, of course," said Lisa. "Silly stuff being blown out of all proportion. But look, we need to handle it now, while it's still small."

"Okay," I said. "I was thinking about doing a post that, you know, gave more context and explained Pearl's actions."

"Sure," said Lisa. "That's certainly an option, but... you know social media is all pretend, right?"

That was worrying. "Well, it's all curated, if that's what you mean."

"Curated, yes," she said. "You choose what to share. And often you have to dumb it down a bit."

"What are you suggesting I do?" I typed.

"It's what you appear to do that's important," said Lisa. "Consider *appearing* to sever all ties with your friend, and apologising for any distress."

"She didn't do anything wrong!"

"Of course not," said Lisa. "It's all playacting. Settle it before it's a thing. I'm sure your friend would agree. You have a long career ahead of you. Throw the monkeys a few bananas."

"Is that really necessary?"

"It's fiction!" said Lisa. "Disavow, apologise, and then maybe do an AMA? Who does it harm?"

"Pearl?"

"She's your friend," said Lisa. "It's just social media. Get her onboard."

"I'll think about it."

"Excellent," said Lisa. "I wouldn't take too long."

Chapter Nine: Questionable Characters.

Was Lisa right? Pearl could be as fictional as Paul, if she needed to be. I mean, I was real, obviously, but convention Pearl, social-media Pearl, didn't have to be. I already knew that she, I, was not going to argue my way out of cancellation. Trans girl, the universal scapegoat. But in this case, I (real Pearl) could sacrifice myself (fake Pearl) to save Paul (also real Pearl). Yes, stupid people would get an apology, but I would know it was a cunning trick.

I couldn't shake the feeling that I was entering a conspiracy with myself but I composed a distancing apology. Lots of "disappointment", reflecting on Pearl's "troubles", hoping for her "growth", "letting her go" as my informal assistant, and finally "not abandoning our long friendship, but adding distance until Pearl has begun to address her anger." I thanked Laios-mouthfeel for bringing it to my attention, though I couldn't resist pointing out that Pearl's pronouns were she/her.

I posted it. The monkeys mostly bought it.

I felt like I had discovered a secret cheat code for life; the ablative persona that could be spun off and abandoned at the first sign of trouble. True, it meant lying and having no shame, but that was a small price. Is this how politicians feel all the time?

"Thank you, Paul," posted Laios-mouthfeel, "for treating this with the seriousness it deserves, and for acting appropriately. Sorry that you had to get involved. (And noted about your ex-assistant's pronouns; if she'd let me know, I would, of course, have used them.)"

"PSA for authors: watch out for delusional men," said MMDrarry. "Paul, you should use his biological pronouns."

"Drarry, shut the fuck up," said Fujojoba.

"Okay, but now PS is free from his assistant; release the sex book!" said Guelfan.

"There really is no sex book!" I wrote. "But I'll be having a Reddit AMA shortly, where I'll be happy to answer questions about the next book."

*
* *

There was probably no point to this, Robb thought, but he drove back to Zdenka's cottage in the forest. His boss could wait.

He was surprised to see another car in the drive, besides Zdenka's battered estate. Generic but hi-performance; he already knew it would be clean and anonymous. A killer's car.

Robb got out of his car; too late for a silent approach. Already a black-suited figure appeared in the cottage's doorway. He was called Jack, Robb knew. A rising star, only a few kills under his belt.

Robb didn't have his hands anywhere near his guns. Jack had a Glock 17, held at his side.

"Hi Jack," Robb said, in a professional tone. "Situation report?"

Chapter Nine: Questionable Characters.

"We thought you were in there," said Jack, cautiously. He felt pretty confident with his gun, thought Robb. Rightly so, probably.

"I began to be a bit suspicious, so I went to check with the boss," Robb lied. "He explained what was going on. Gave me an option to get back in his good graces. Am I too late?"

"The boss wanted you to kill the primary target?" said Jack. "We thought there was something between you."

"There was," said Robb. "Pretty torn up, but a job's a job, right? Did you kill him?"

"Not yet. It's just... we have instructions to kill you as well," said Jack, almost apologetically.

"The boss said he'd ring and update you," said Robb. Jack glanced towards where his phone was secreted.

Robb dived over the hood of the car, disappearing behind it.

"Shit," muttered Jack. The crunch of gravel indicated that he was going prone to look, and shoot, beneath the car. But Robb was crouched with a wheel obscuring his legs.

More gravel noises from Jack; getting to his feet, cautiously edging round the front of the cars. Robb took the few seconds as an opportunity to slip into the woods.

"Fuck," said Jack. Careful not to drop his aim, Jack pulled something from a belt pouch. Night vision goggles. That wasn't good, thought Robb. Just light amplification, not thermal, which was a plus though.

Robb threw himself down into a shadowy dip in the terrain. Technically, Jack was making a mistake; he should have fallen back to the cottage. But this would be cold comfort if he shot Robb.

Jack edged into the woods, cautiously. The light amplification would help him, but he still needed to pick up human shapes; that was why Robb was lying and not crouching. Robb carefully felt for the key fob, and locked the car.

At the beep and clunk, Jack turned, and Robb launched himself. While he was still turning, Jack realised what was happening and turned back, but Robb tackled him and they both went over. They rolled over the leaf litter and brambles. Jack tried to bring his gun to bear, but Robb had his knee on Jack's wrist, and head-butted him. Jack didn't quite lose consciousness, but was dazed enough for Robb to take his gun and jam it under Jack's chin.

"Sitrep?" Robb hissed, again.

Jack hesitated and then obviously gave up. "There's a panic room," he said. "Vaughan reckons it's prosumer, but hi-grade. York is looking for improvised explosives. Lynton is down."

"Down? How?" said Robb.

"Zdenka," said Jack. "She got the target to the safe room. She's injured."

Robb knocked Jack out, and headed for the cottage.

Chapter Nine: Questionable Characters.

***

In my keenness to avoid cancellation I had given myself three fresh problems; one, I had to work out what the next book was (I had written nothing decent in months). Two, I needed a Reddit login; I didn't go there. It was worse than Tumblr. And three, Pippin would have to pose for one of those ask me anything validation pictures. Which shouldn't be a problem, except that he hadn't been home in a few days. He'd gotten back with Dean (and Dean's wife and children had moved out).

I messaged Beatrice. "Hi Beatrice," I said. "Can we talk about the next book?"

"Of course, Paul," Beatrice said. "Have you got a draft to show me?"

"Um, no," I said. Lately I have had no taste for writing. No excitement. But these things go in cycles. "I'm... wondering if it is what you are expecting. I mean, if you had to guess?"

"Well, different main characters; Obviously, it's too awkward to have them break up and get back together. It can be done, but the market won't like that," said Beatrice. "But it should be the same universe. I'd say promote one of the other characters, but you actually don't have many other male characters."

"I was thinking Vaughan?"

"Hang on," said Beatrice. She was almost certainly searching the text. She was gone for a while, then, "No, I wouldn't do that."

"Why not?"

"Vaughan is Black and now disabled," Beatrice said. "Some of your audience won't like that."

"Which bit?"

"Either or both. And those that do like it, will grumble about Own Voices," said Beatrice. "Unless...?"

"No."

"Probably for the best," said Beatrice. "The market dislikes those characteristics."

"People—racist and/or ableist people—dislike those characteristics," I said.

"I concern myself with the ocean, not the droplets," said Beatrice. The unexpected poetry of this meant that it took me a few seconds to realise it was a verbal shrug.

"So, should I just pick another hired killer? A white and non-disabled one?" I said.

"Exactly," said Beatrice. "Or rewrite Vaughan slightly; no-one will notice."

"No-one will notice his arm has grown back, and he's now white?"

"As long as you don't tell anyone," said Beatrice. "Look, this is the sort of dark secret writers usually take a few books to work out, but readers ignore ninety percent of your descriptions."

"I'd like to think my readers pay attention."

"Yes, every new author does," said Beatrice. "And then, for the other side of the romance, doesn't Peter have a brother? Or a cousin?"

Chapter Nine: Questionable Characters.

"Wouldn't that mean I'm just writing the same book again?"

"Nothing wrong with that!" said Beatrice, "especially in romance. But if you want to get clever; Peter's cousin is the strong man with big hands, and your killer is the waif-like twink."

Oh shit, that would work. I could force myself to write that. "Our killer is a lonely sniper, our prince is a popular rugby player," I said.

"Excellent," said Beatrice. "Write a few chapters and I can gauge interest."

Okay, I could bullshit about book two.

And making a Reddit login was fine; they didn't make you promise to be annoying, so I guess it's voluntary.

Pippin finally got home. He was a bit out of it, but agreeable. I had made an AMA sign out of an A4 pad.

"So just hold it up, right?" Pippen said, holding the sign in front of his face.

"With your face showing."

Pippin lowered the sign. "This is boring though," he said. "Can I James Bond it?"

"How?"

Pippin sprinted to his room and came back with a hairdryer. He pretended to shoot it, making pew-pew noises. I sighed; men.

"The photo," I reminded him.

He posed, 'gun' in one hand, the sign in the other. I snapped a pic. The kitchen was a bit cluttered, but I was sure that a little informal would be fine.

"Hi, I'm Paul Sisters, the author of Muzzle and Escutcheon, the exciting new M/M crime-romance out now from Apollo Flings. #AskMeAnything."

Chapter Ten: Rotten Girl.

I think authors sometimes overestimate the degree to which their readers want novelty. At least, I hoped they did, as I pitched a sequel that was a simple re-skin of the original.

I don't know, perhaps it's okay. If I order a toasted cheese sandwich, I'm not disappointed that it is very similar to the last toasted cheese sandwich. Perhaps our hunger for mental stimulation was much the same. But if I was making those sandwiches, I know I'd be tempted to try different sorts of cheese, different sorts of mayo. This line of thought was making me hungry.

"Sure!" I typed. "We're staying in the crime-filled world of contractors and hitmen. Valentine is a sniper; distant and slight, going through life in a cloud of dullness and death. George is a rugby player with a cheery demeanour, more at home on the field or as a volunteer in a soup kitchen than in the high-flying world he was born to. But when they meet; balls and bullets fly!"

They were asking about the next book. I had been insanely nervous, but the AMA was going well. Plain cheese and cheap mayonnaise was enough for this crowd. A few more questions and I could make my escape.

A Rotten Girl

"Are you definitely a man?" asked a user called Yaoi-gourmet, out of nowhere. It is unusual to ask a cis person—like Paul—this, but my secret trans training meant I was used to it.

"Er, rude. But yes." I sighed. I didn't like to write this, but, "I checked in the bathroom last time I had a pee." Yes, yes, I was speaking their language; pretending that having a dick made you male.

"Have you heard about the spate of M/M authors pretending to be men, but really being women?"

"Um, I know it happens, yeah," I said. "And really, as long as the story is good, it's not the end of the world."

I got downvoted quite heavily on that.

"Anyhow," I typed. "In my case, the readers who saw me at Aphrowriting can confirm it though, I think."

"And are you gay?" asked Yaoi-gourmet.

"Yes, and proud of it," I said. "I can't really prove that though!"

"Did you enjoy the Aphrowriting Con?" asked someone. I was glad to change the subject.

"Ah, sunny Birmingham," I replied. "It was a bit scary, but it was lovely meeting readers, as well as other writers. I had a great time."

"There seems to be some confusion about whether this is your first book," said someone else.

"Not from me!" I said. "I mean, I've been writing since I was a kid, but this is definitely my first published book."

Chapter Ten: Rotten Girl.

"Your assistant seems to have thought you did," said user GuelFan, who I assume was the same as the Twitter Guelfan.

"Pearl gets a bit confused sometimes," I said. "And she didn't have a good weekend."

"If you're gay," asked Yaoi-gourmet. "Why did you share your hotel room with a woman?"

"Because they're expensive? And Pearl is a friend," I typed. "She likes women, and I like men. You're being rather silly."

"But Pearl's a man," said a user named JKDNW.

"No, she's a woman," I said. "A trans woman."

"I suppose it's alright if Pearl is a man," commented Yaoi-gourmet.

"No, she's a woman, a lesbian," I said, beginning to lose my temper. "I'm a gay man. We've known each other for ages. We can share the same room with no impropriety. This isn't the 1800s!"

"You seemed to dump her pretty easily, though," said a random user. "She is no longer your assistant, right?"

"She was never really my assistant," I said. "It was all informal. And, yes, she had a bad weekend, but I'm not going to discuss her personal life."

"Did you know about the assault?" asked JKDNW.

"What assault?" I typed. I was furious.

"He assaulted a young woman in her room," said JKDNW.

"No, she didn't," I said. "There was a misunderstanding. She accidentally broke a coffee cup. That's it!"

"How do you know?" said JKDNW. "Taking his word for it? You've already proven you're gullible by believing his stupid pronouns." That comment seemed to be downvoted a fair bit, but not enough.

"I'm not arguing with a transphobe," I said.

"The character of Zdenka always seemed a little trans coded to me. I wondered, is Zdenka trans?" asked a random Emily. How was I supposed to answer that?

"No," I responded. I felt bad, but this whole trans debacle was messing things up. Paul was cis. I needed to remember that. He was an ally, sure, but we know what allies are like. "If the way she's written resounds in you, that's the important part. I'm not trans so I can't possibly do justice to a trans character. And probably shouldn't. Trans rights, and all, but I should leave that to the trans writers."

I ended the AMA there. I was tired of this bullshit.

*
**

Twitter was abuzz again. I should just leave it, but I didn't have the willpower.

On the plus side there was a lot of chat about the second book, which was good. I still had to write it, and I didn't feel much like writing. But still, I was beginning to think that it wasn't so bad. I was wrong.

Chapter Ten: Rotten Girl.

"Is the questionable Pearl actually Pearl Camellia?" asked Guelfan. "A wannabe writer?"

"Based on what?" said Fujojoba. "The same first name? It's not that unusual."

"Paul mentioned the book was Tattoo-something," said Guelfan. "And Camellia wrote a book called Transient Tattoo."

"So, the wrong name, written by the wrong person," said Fujojoba. "It's beyond thin, Sherlock. Has this person got any pictures?"

No, I hadn't. I'm not stupid. Guelfan didn't respond. I thought about locking Pearl's—er, my—account, but that seemed rather obvious.

I made myself a toasted cheese sandwich. This was good because I needed food, and bad because I was too anxious to taste it. It wasn't a very original toasted cheese sandwich anyway.

"Ha, knew it," posted Guelfan, along with two pictures. The first was my AMA picture of Paul/Pippin. The second was a zoomed in section showing the kettle, and me taking the photo. It was blurred, distorted by the kettle's curve, and the phone hid my face.

"That's her," said Laios-mouthfeel. "But I thought Paul was distancing himself from her." At least Laios-mouthfeel was using the right pronouns.

***

York didn't even hear Robb approaching. Robb had never rated York highly; he was brutal and inefficient. He was taping a couple of propane tanks together; Robb knocked him out with the butt of his pistol.

Robb poked his head into the sitting room, taking in the wall panel that must have hidden the safe room door, Lynton's body, the vault-like safe room door, and Vaughan bringing up a shotgun; a Benelli M4 Tactical.

Robb dived out of the doorway, as a section of door frame disintegrated. Vaughan was, by speciality, a sniper, but he preferred a shotgun for house-clearing. Robb rated him highly; he was calm and an excellent shot. The organisation seemed less keen; possibly because Escutcheon was old-fashioned, and had very few Black operatives.

Robb crawled quickly, putting space and a kitchen counter between them.

"Robb?" Vaughan called. "I thought it was strange that you weren't shooting at us. Come out and surrender, and we'll see what the boss has to say."

"Yeah, unfortunately Jack already told me you have orders to kill me," said Robb.

"Damn," said Vaughan with a chuckle. "Newbies, eh? I'm sorry about this. No hard feelings, yeah?"

Vaughan shot at Robb's position, into the counter. Vaughan was no newbie; he remembered that guns could shoot through things. Robb kicked himself for replying. It was sheer dumb luck that whatever was in this counter

Chapter Ten: Rotten Girl.

(small appliance? cast-iron pot? Zdenka's emergency kevlar supply?) had managed to protect him.

Robb pulled out his phone, and set an alarm for one minute, and popped it in the counter cupboard. He heard Vaughan's footsteps. Robb crawled away, manoeuvring—like a squirrel on a tree trunk—to keep out of Vaughan's sight.

When Robb's alarm went off, Vaughan immediately fired into the cupboard. Robb launched himself over the counter, kicking the shotgun out of Vaughan's hands. Vaughan immediately punched Robb; it would have been in his solar plexus, but he managed to turn in time. Robb kicked out, but Vaughan was backing off, and reaching inside his jacket. Robb lunged for the fallen shotgun, and—grabbing it—turned and fired. Vaughan's arm was blown away; he fell backwards.

"Sorry," said Robb. "I'll call an ambulance as I leave."

"Dead from blood loss by then," said Vaughan, neutrally. "Use my tie as a tourniquet."

Cautiously but quickly, Robb removed Vaughan's tie and fastened it around his upper arm.

Robb hurried to the safe room, looking around for a camera. "Peter, Zdenka, it's safe now."

With a set of loud clunks, the door opened.

"Robb, thank heavens," said Peter. "Zdenka's badly hurt."

A Rotten Girl

Zdenka was lying in an enormous pool of blood, barely conscious.

"Robb," she whispered. "You're finally here. I protected your boy. You owe me." She closed her eyes.

"Z, we'll get you an ambulance—"

"Phones are jammed. Anyway, I wouldn't make it," said Zdenka. "At least I didn't have to see Peter fire my gun. Look after each other."

"Robb," said Peter. "Do something!"

Zdenka smiled, and died in front of them.

Peter and Robb hugged each other.

Then Robb heard the sound of a helicopter.

***

"Okay, okay," typed Fujojoba. "So Paul said he wrote a book with Tattoo in the name, under a pseudonym, but Pearl wrote something Tattoo. What's going on?"

Guelfan said, "I think Paul used Pearl's name to publish his first book, rather than making up a name. But he now wants to pretend he didn't. Anyone know what the book is about?"

"The impermanence of modern life on the margins, apparently," said MMDrarry. "Sounds like shit."

"I've bought it," said Laios-mouthfeel. Yay, a sale, I suppose. "It's all trans stuff. Slice of life, I suppose. Extremely overwritten and boring. Who wants to read

Chapter Ten: Rotten Girl.

about just lesbians, even if they're trans? The author must have been going for a male audience."

"Trans bullshit," said MMDrarry. "I knew it."

"But Paul just said that only trans people should write trans books," said Guelfan. "That doesn't make sense."

"Is Paul trans?" said Fujojoba.

"Why is the book from a trans woman's POV?" said Laios-mouthfeel.

"Detransitioner," said MMDrarry. "Happens to nearly 100% of trans identified people." Only wrong by 99 percent, MMDrarry.

"So, he was a man, turned into a woman, and then back into a man?" said Guelfan.

"He was a man who was delusional for a bit, then got over it," said MMDrarry.

"Oh," said Guelfan. "So in the end, he is a man who writes M/M. Not an imposter."

"Yay! That makes sense," said Laios-mouthfeel. "Is that right, Paul? Are you a detransitioner?" And she at-ed me.

Well, this certainly wasn't ideal. But I suppose sometimes a character leads you in an unexpected direction.

"Okay," Paul posted. "I suppose I should come clean. Yes, I am a detransitioner; I have nothing against trans people but it wasn't for me. People have the right to self-identify, and that means that a tiny percentage of us get it wrong."

"Kudos for finally seeing through their lies," said MMDrarry. "But boo for still kowtowing to their stupid cult. They are threatening you aren't they?"

"FFS Drarry, try to be normal," said Fujojoba.

"Paul, has this put a bit of distance between you and Pearl?" asked Laios-mouthfeel, obviously appointing herself counsellor. Sorry, Pearl, you get to be universal scapegoat again.

"Yes, LM, I think maybe that's true," I said. "Pearl and I are old friends, and to start with seemed to have similar paths ahead of us. But as my path diverged from hers, an element of animosity has entered our relationship."

"In other words, you began to see what a porn-addled tranny he is," said MMDrarry. I blocked her. I should have before.

"That sounds like it's quite troubling, Paul," said Laios-mouthfeel. "But it explains why there was an odd tension between you two. And also perhaps why Pearl behaved oddly."

Fuck off. "Yes," I typed. "You might be right. Me and Pearl go back a long way, but maybe our paths have diverged too much."

"Hang on," said Guelfan. "Who wrote Transient Tattoo then? And why do you both think it's bad?"

Bloody hell. Um. "We both did," I typed. "I did most of the writing, but Pearl was really the subject. You can tell because the main character likes girls. I was already starting to feel I'd made a mistake, so, in the end it made

Chapter Ten: Rotten Girl.

sense for Pearl's name to be on the cover. Neither of us was happy with the result."

"Oh Paul," said Laios-mouthfeel. "Thank you for being honest with us. I know it must have been difficult, but we're here for you."

"Why don't you and Pearl follow each other on Twitter?" asked Fujojoba.

"As I say, things have gotten rather unfriendly between us," I said. "It makes me very sad."

"But you let her photograph you for the AMA?" said Fujojoba.

"Well, someone needed too," I said. "And we're still flatmates." Oh, I could use the truth here. "And finding another place for a similar rent is next to impossible. Pearl's mother is the landlord, and she gives us both a major break."

"Trying to summon the ghost of Mao," said Fujojoba.

"That sounds terrible, Paul," said Laios-mouthfeel. "We're all with you."

Okay, I think that's it; no more awkward questions to explain.

"I'm confused," asked a user called SimonAtDalby. "Why haven't you got a dick?"

Oh, for fuck's sake. Bloody Simon. Also, very rude. I think trans people must have a badge that says, "Hi! Ask me about my genitals," that is only visible to cis people.

I could just lie and say I have a dick. I mean, that's not a lie for me, Pearl, or for Paul, but it is for Pippin. But Simon isn't going to have any proof, and was on

159

A Rotten Girl

(apparently mid) drugs at the time. Unless he does have proof? Or he is a convincing speaker. Fuck, the truth is better; well, the material truth, and then some more lies.

"I didn't fully realise that I'd made a mistake until after I'd had my bottom surgery," I said. "So, while I would prefer not to discuss this online, I have a neo-vagina."

"You let them cut off your dick before you realised that was a bad idea?" said MMDrarry2. "No wonder you're cross with them." I blocked her again.

"It is not 'cutting off'," I said. "The surgery is quite advanced." I had looked into it, in an 'if I won the lottery' way.

"Hang on, doesn't that mean he is a girl?" said Guelfan. "Drarry said men have penises, so I assume..."

"Drarry is an idiot," said Fujojoba.

"Oh," said SimonAtDalby. "If you'd have said that, it would have been fine. I'm bisexual."

"We say pansexual now," said Laios-mouthfeel, wrongly.

***

Some of the Romance blogs picked up on this. Most got a couple of parts wrong, but general consensus was:
- Paul is a gay man. (Applause.)
- Who is a detransitioner. (Confused clapping and boos.)
- Who hasn't got a dick. (Boos.)
- But he writes M/M. (Applause.)

Chapter Ten: Rotten Girl.

- And at least one of his characters has a big dick. (Wild applause.)

I was happy enough with that; most people seemed fairly accepting. Imagining an unwanted bottom surgery was triggering my dysphoria, but that couldn't be helped. And the transfem ancestor spirits had turned their backs on me, but they—in the manner of such things—were fictional.

Laios-mouthfeel and SimonAtDalby both sent me direct messages, wondering if I would be at any future cons. I said I didn't think so. This was true; I don't think I could take the stress.

The-Hated-Authortrix posted a link to one of the blogs, "Fujoshis being very normal this afternoon."

I relaxed for the first time in hours.

* * *

I was awakened by the front door slamming.

"What the fuck is this?" Pippin said. I don't think I have ever seen him so angry.

"What?"

"I am not a detransitioner!" he said.

"No," I said, gathering myself. "But Paul is."

"Paul isn't real," said Pippin. "But my photos are."

"You were okay with pretending to be cis," I said. "Detrans is just cis with a detour."

A Rotten Girl

"I don't want to be detrans," said Pippin. He was standing, pacing. "And I hate the idea of having the wrong sort of bottom surgery. What kind of idiot is Paul?"

"It's all fiction," I said. "But things got a bit out of hand."

"Out of hand?" Pippin said. "Do you have any idea how difficult it was to explain to Dean? He's a dad, Pearl; his brain isn't built for this."

"How does Dean know?" I asked.

"He read it in *IRN View*!" Indie Romance News View was a Scottish Indie Rom blog. Hardly the sort of tabloid a dad should be reading. I said as much.

"He likes romance!" said Pippin. "He's not a stereotype." All Pippin's sexual partners were stereotypes, but now was not the time to say that.

"I shouldn't have said yes," said Pippin. "There's nothing wrong with being trans. Why did you have to lie about everything?"

"It's fiction, not lies!" I said. "And people are finally reading me."

"Reading Paul," said Pippin.

"I'm Paul."

"You're Pearl," said Pippin. "You're even mean to yourself; letting people get away with saying crap."

"That's fictional Pearl," I said. "She doesn't matter."

"Are you sure?" he said. "It ends now."

"No, I've just finally got everyone convinced."

"Until the next time," Pippin said. "Isn't Paul writing another book?"

Chapter Ten: Rotten Girl.

"I intend to, yes," I said. "It's so much easier as a man."

Pippin sighed. "Have some fucking pride," he said. "You've betrayed me, you've betrayed Barbara, you've even betrayed yourself. No more."

"But—"

"Tell everyone," said Pippin, "or I will."

"No—"

"Fine," said Pippin. He went to his room and slammed the door.

***

Pippin's notes/apology was fairly concise. He said that I was pretending to be Paul, and that he was the face of Paul. He apologised for his part in the deception. I couldn't be bothered to fight him. I could have said that he was crazy, a troll, a stalker. But that was only delaying the inevitable.

The Scooby Gang (Laios-mouthfeel, Guelfan, Fujojoba and MMDrarry3) worked out most of the details. That was particularly annoying. It was like the denouement of a *Columbo* episode, except that Columbo had decided that you weren't worth it, and so had his basset hound do the investigation. Did you know his dog was called 'Dog'?

I sold a few more copies on the mini-controversy, but then sales dropped off precipitously.

Lisa sent a short "disappointed" email. Apparently, honesty is a thing publishers are definitely into.

Beatrice also dropped me. "The market is currently about authenticity, Pearl," she wrote, somehow getting my name right. "And as the old joke goes; if you can fake that you've got it made."

"I thought that was sincerity?" I said.

"Well, that's a problem too," she said, which was fair.

My mom complained that I was calling her a landlord. She'd prefer "independent housing provisioner."

I just sat in my room and let everything collapse around me. Girlrotted. I should have known that the taste of respect, of readership, of fandom even, would be fleeting. For an instant I thought it—my grail—was graspable, but my fingers just scrabbled against its gilt surface for a few seconds before I fell. The reflection of a beautiful cis girl for a moment, before the rot became apparent.

Respect wasn't something trans women got or deserved. Oh, maybe there were one or two, usually posh, always passable, but they were still clinging on with their fingernails. *This is for cis people, male people, they said, not you.* They had destroyed trans women way more innocent and more talented than I.

The fujoshi hated me. Actually, more because I confused and embarrassed them than anything else. They tolerated a lot of women writing M/M, after all. Plus, a sizable proportion thought I was 'male enough', which is exactly what every trans girl longs to hear. But they would never forgive me for making them look like clowns. Even if they bought the long shoes and greasepaint themselves.

Chapter Ten: Rotten Girl.

My own clan, the trans girls, also hated me. Because I had brought them into disrepute. Because I had not behaved with honour. Because I was disloyal. I couldn't argue.

The wider queer community, in the few instances when it became aware of me, also hated me. From the broadest cliques (gay men) to the narrowest (transmasc uwus working for defence contractors), all could find something to hate me for.

At least society as a whole continued to hate me for being trans; no offence was necessary, and no forgiveness would ever be forthcoming.

Chapter Eleven: The End.

In classic, angsty novels, things sometimes reach a point when the only way out is death. Self-inflicted death. I'm thinking Anna Karenina; I can see how, "... escape from everyone and from myself," is appealing. Or, like my girl Emma Bovary, "I shall fall asleep and all will be over."

It's tidy, from an authorial point of view. Also from a personal point of view; people will say stuff about 'those you leave behind,' but why the hell would a dead person care? How would they care?

Well, sorry to disappoint, but I'm not going to Karenina myself. Knowing me, I'd probably get a rail replacement bus service, anyway.

I am one of those red dots on an aeroplane diagram; damaged but alive. Unfortunately, being trans in this society is a dangerous business. All of us that are still alive have lost someone. And we know it's not virtue or determination or fucking bravery that allows us to continue. It's dumb luck, and maybe some material help. Or maybe the long and short of it was that I am too scared of pain.

Barbs told me that she had come close in her teenage years. She was going to open her wrists in the forest. What

A Rotten Girl

stopped her was considering how relieved her parents would be. So I guess it is worth thinking about 'those you leave behind', after all. *If you're trans you have to live*, this, in the end, is close to an article of faith for me. We are too few, and have too many enemies, to let ourselves lose anyone. And no-one wants to make terfs smile.

I have left the house at least. Pippin still isn't really talking to me; the odd word, when it's absolutely necessary. I headed for nature, stomping through the bluebells.

Mum had gotten angry with my inaction, my 'laziness'. She had visited, but I had locked myself in my room, as if regressing to my teenage years. She had a long but inaudible conversation with Pippin.

Dad rang with his 'advice'; mum must have told him. His advice boiled down to two things, which he said have served him well. One, tell everyone and anyone that you're not bullshitting them. People mistrust bullshitters, so they are always glad to hear someone say they aren't one. Two, don't be a girl.

I hung up on him.

What finally got me out of the house were some DM notifications from Barbs. I didn't read them. They would, undoubtedly, have made me feel better, but also angry that she was bothering. Ashamed that she had to. And sad that I've lost her. I left my phone behind.

So I came to her favourite place in the park, and stared out over the water. It was a sunny day, but the pool was still boring.

Chapter Eleven: The End.

I sat on that fallen log, anyway. People walked into the ocean, but I didn't think this pool would do. I'd just end up sitting up to my waist in mud. Another one-star Goodreads review for my attempted offing. And anyway, I'd ruin the place for Barbs. That was one betrayal I could not commit.

And annoyingly Pippin was right; there were already enough betrayals. But I really had been prepared to ruin everything I loved to get the respect of cis folk. Even you, gentle and imaginary reader; I didn't tell you who wrote the negative Transient Tattoo review did I? Take a guess. I hoped I could get some buzz off the sexism.

The question is, if Pippin hadn't unmasked me, would I ever have stopped the deception? Would I do it again?

What kind of person hesitates at that question? I am clearly an incomplete tran; my trans acquaintances are resolute and full of pride and self-determination, but I seem to have missed out. I just want praise from some of the stupidest people in the world.

At least it was relaxing watching the water, though. Never really still; its surface wrinkled by passing ducks and trailing branches. An imperfect mirror to the sky and the surrounding leaves. There was only a light wind, but everything moved; the water, the trees, the bluebells. Not in synchrony, but not independently either. Like a community, perhaps.

Some of the ducks were the fancy ones; a vorticist plumage full of clashing gradients. Barbs would know what they were called. That always struck me as a useless skill—knowing the specific types of natural shit—but I really missed those snippets of information. I wish I knew what those tall trees with ridged oval leaves were; swaying ponderously and occasionally shaking in a random gust of wind. The trees that languorously trailed their leaves in the water were weeping willows, right? Or had I just made that up? I supposed it didn't matter; against my will, the soft splashing and gentle birdsong was relaxing me.

I had set the end of *Muzzle and Escutcheon* here. It is always easier to use real places. Zdenka's cottage was the holiday let in Wales that we stayed in when I was nine or ten. Marcia, Trevor and I in a Welsh forest; neither of the adults liked nature, and I think they had begun to realise they didn't like each other either. Shitty holiday. But good scenery.

I pictured Robb and Peter stumbling out of the forest.

*
* *

Robb and Peter stumbled out of the forest. The pool in front of them was not huge, but was an obstacle that Robb would have preferred not to run into. On a quiet walk, this would be a nice place to stop. He and Peter could sit on that fallen log, and look at the trees and the water. Listen to the gentle song of the forest. Kiss. Robb turned left, still holding Peter's hand.

A burst of automatic fire chewed up the leaves ahead of him.

Chapter Eleven: The End.

"Stop!" The voice was modulated, disguised, but familiar. Robb's boss, Mr Herald. "It would be very rude to just kill you without speaking first."

Robb turned. Four men and his boss. At least, he assumed as much; Mr Herald rarely did field work. Robb had always spoken to him over telephone or intercom. He wore a sharp, black suit, and a blackened full-face respirator mask. Robb had seen some of the goons before; excellent and well-armed. It didn't look like they were going to get their quiet walk.

"Drop your guns, Mr Casement," said his boss. "My guards are aiming at Peter, so don't try anything smart."

"Why?" said Robb. "You are going to kill us, anyway. Why don't I see how many I can take with me?"

"Because you're a good operative—one I'm sorry to lose—and you know that an extra five-minute chat is a chance for unexpected opportunities to arise," said Mr Herald.

Robb swore. "Okay," he said, and began dropping his weapons.

"Now move away," said his boss.

A single guard was dispatched, and—with some hesitation—he patted Robb down. The guard then stuffed the guns in a carry-all, and walked back to the boss.

"I'll take it from here," said Mr Herald to his guards. "Fall back to the helicopter."

Robb weighed up the distance between them.

"No, Mr Casement," Mr Herald said. "I could shoot both of you before you got to me." He had a pistol, a Glock 19.

"Anyhow, isn't it nicer to have a private conversation?" Mr Herald pulled off his mask. "Away from the guards."

"Father?" said Peter.

"Lord Glearbury?" said Robb.

"Sorry about this whole inconvenience," said Mr Herald. "Peter, you especially. Killing one's son is quite vulgar."

"Father," stammered Peter. "What are you doing?"

"I have nothing against homosexuals, you understand," he said. "Robb will tell you; Escutcheon hires all sorts of deviants. But it won't do for a family of the Ukebridge-Talbot's history and legacy."

"So you're going to kill him?" said Robb.

"That is largely your fault," said Mr Herald. "Originally, I hired another team to kidnap him, quietly. Arranged marriage used to be a noble tradition, you know. Cecelia was onboard. But you caused too much of a kerfuffle; so it was more efficient to hire my own agency, in secret, to tidy up the situation."

"And kill us?" said Peter.

"Yes. Simpler all round," said Mr Herald. "Your brother is a bit of a fool, but I'm sure he'll be a pliable spare. If it helps, the press will definitely speculate about gayness underlying your upcoming murder-suicide. Any last words?"

"You are a terrible father," said Peter.

Chapter Eleven: The End.

"Worse than mine," said Robb, "and that's saying something."

"A lord's first duty is to the family as a whole," said Lord Glearbury. "Not individual members. Farewell, son."

He raised the gun. A shot rang out.

***

A branch snapped behind me.

What the fuck was I doing out without my phone? Now I was going to get hatecrimed to death. That was even worse than suicide.

"Hiya." It was Barbs. She looked a little nervous.

Her very existence astonished me. Too many people in my life have been fictional, lately. "How did you find me?"

She shrugged. "Seemed likely. You should answer your phone." She sat down on the fallen log, and got out a pack of biscuits. "Bicky?"

Oh no. I was going to cry. I was going to cry in front of her. "I'm sorry," I said. "I'm sorry." She pulled me in and held me while I sobbed.

The birdsong and lapping water continued. She was right; nature didn't care. The trees didn't know about terfs, the water didn't care about crimance, the ducks didn't know what fujoshis were. Well, probably. You could never tell with ducks. I laughed through my sobs.

"What's up?" said Barbs.

"What are those ducks?" I said. "The showy ones."

A Rotten Girl

"Mandarin ducks," said Barbs. "Moderately rare. That's the drakes you're looking at, the hens are the modest grey-brown ducks with the cunty eyeshadow."

"God, can you imagine how crap it is to be a trans duck?" I said.

"That's why man is the paragon of animals," said Barbs. "Eyeshadow."

We ate biscuits in silence for a bit.

"Barbs," I said, after a while. "You didn't really say when you went away... And I know I don't deserve it..."

"Fuck 'deserve it'," said Barbs. "Is Paul gone?"

"Yes."

"Well good," she said, squeezing me. "Guess you weren't the only one worried about exclusivity."

"But I did so many bad things," I said. "The transfem sisterhood has cancelled me, and rightly so. You will catch strays from that."

"I'll manage," said Barbs.

"And... and I still don't know if I'm immune to... the market," I said. "I mean, I have to make money; I can't completely forget about that."

"Yep, we live in capitalism," said Barbs. "It isn't practical to withdraw from it, if you want to survive. But you also can't let it capture you. So you have to stay somewhere between those two points."

"Sounds like centrism."

"Centrism is a trap," said Barbs, "with an invisible ratchet taking you step-by-step into the beast's maw. We have to be guerrillas, ninjas, vampires. Supping from the

Chapter Eleven: The End.

beast when it is mostly safe to do so, but never forgetting it is the enemy."

"I'm not sure I'm cut out for a vampire's life," I said.

"Don't worry, you can still eat garlic."

"But seriously," I said, "what if I get no readers?"

"You will always have at least one reader."

"I should probably actually listen to you more, eh?"

***

Zdenka's pistol was a Beretta Tomcat 3032. Silver and black, incredibly small. Peter's arm shook.

Lord Glearbury toppled over backwards, a bullet through his eye and skull. Robb was impressed, but didn't think, 'Good job on killing your dad,' would be appreciated right now.

Robb gently took the gun from Peter's hand, and fired a shot into Mr Herald's torso.

"If his men are listening for shots, they would be expecting two," he explained. They might be able to tell the difference between a Glock and a Beretta, but Robb suspected not.

He pulled Peter in towards him, and kissed him quickly. "We've got to run now, Lord Peter," he said. "But the company will crumble in a couple of hours without your— without Mr Herald at the helm."

Peter nodded, and hand in hand they walked into the forest.

***

We kissed, and walked back through the park, hand in hand except whenever we came near other people.

"Any thoughts as to what you are going to write next?" asked Barbs

"Not sure," I said, realising that I was actually excited about writing again. "I'm definitely going to write something trans-focused though."

"Excellent," said Barbs.

"I could make real enemies and have Peter and Robb admit their egginess. Their growing feeling that they are both transgender, both girls," I said.

"Oh, the M/M contingent would lose their minds," said Barbs.

"With Peter inheriting the estate, and the remains of Escutcheon, they certainly have the money," I said. "At least they wouldn't have to wait for the NHS. But doing it amidst a war between the mercenary companies might be almost as hard."

"Yeah," said Barbs, chuckling.

"But I'm probably going to leave all that behind," I said. "Do something fun and stupid. Space pirates, monster-fucking, or similar. Please the transfem ancestor spirits."

"Ever think of writing about this whole thing?" Barbs said. "Paul, publishing, etc?"

Chapter Eleven: The End.

"Fuck no," I said. "I already overuse dialogue; paraphrasing Twitter convos and WhatsApp messages would make for ridiculously tedious reading."

We released hands as we passed by a couple on a bench, holding them again as we rounded the next corner.

"Plus, Pippin still hasn't forgiven me," I said.

"He's a man," said Barbs. "They are either vicious chihuahuas or dopey labradors. You know which Pippin is. He will probably forget soon."

"And the rest of the world?" I said. "I don't want to have to start again."

"You're a trans girl," said Barbs. "It's in our nature to restart. In my line of work, we call it iteration. Most people just take the first puberty they are assigned, after all, but not us."

She was right, of course. We iterated ourselves into the body, the identity, even the life that we wanted. Maybe that was an uphill journey on a rocky trail, or a swim against a current of foetid transphobia, but we kept going. I hugged Barbs. Things might be shitty now, but now is not the end.

~~The End~~

Acknowledgements

Thank you for reading.

Special thanks to Benjanun Sriduangkaew for prompting me to write something outside my comfort zone!

Thanks to Amelia, Angelica, Carmilla and Celeste, for everything.

And thanks to my excellent reading team, particularly Bee, Clockwork Sapphire, Princess ChooChoo, and ViviAnne for their sterling work.

Thanks, again, to my friends amongst the dead: Lyndon and Marie. And to Ben, for getting me here.

~Jemma

(jemmatopaz.carrd.co)

v1.08p

Other Books by this Author

Writing as Jemma Topaz

As Happy as Pirates or Burglars
(Pirates and Tyrants 1)

Taisiya is a jewel thief in a fantastic future: she doesn't need the jewels but she certainly needs the challenge. So when she encounters a desirable Pirate Captain...

A high-heat lesbian space adventure with bondage, discipline, and submission.

Captains of a Tyrant Fate
(Pirates and Tyrants 2)

Melesina, a scion of an Imperial star system, finds that the assassination of her father didn't go at all as she planned. She is now politely fighting for her life in a court full of cunning nobles and wily spies.

Meanwhile, her trans sister Nada is just having fun, most of it carnal; but her past resurfaces, and she must choose whether to return to face danger and doubt.

Among the rest of the crew, hobbyist thief Taisiya also has difficulties: sharing her mind with a new headmate.

Can she work with the ruthless Imperial operative in her brain, or will she get betrayed again?

A high-heat sapphic sci-fi adventure with lesbians, robots, and spaceships!

Our Monsters
(Terat 1)

Rosemary Dulahan, answering a strange job posting, arrives in Monstertown – a place inhabited by magical beings from another world.

Navigating the politics of sphinxes, lamias, and secrets, she must learn how to get along with her non-human coworkers and maybe romance a few monster girls along the way.

There's nothing she wants less than getting caught up in a murder mystery troubling all of Monstertown... but the mystery doesn't care what she wants, and she's about to discover the darker side of her new world.

The Brute of Greengrave
(and other stories of witches and dolls, mortals and beasts)

Peer into a world of mysterious witches and deadly dolls, of ferocious hellhounds, faerie beast-women, and poor, ordinary mortals. A trans lesbian focused collection of ten interlinked stories of occult mystery.

- **The Brute of Greengrave** - at an arcane fox hunt, a young witch wrestles with her nobility and cruelty.
- **Predatory Finance** - a trans employee and her cis boss start an ill-advised relationship; will money, power and risk overcome their circumstances?
- **With Anguish Moist and Fever-dew** - a thief pretends to be a maid for a noble witch, but there are more secrets in this house than the thief suspects.

...and more such tales!

Tempting Poison
(stories of toxic and broken lesbians)

Thirteen tales of toxic lesbians, too hot for Amazon!

Ranging from ancient and cruel vampire countesses through to modern-day corporate businesswomen, and on to cool and futuristic dommes, this collection has a range of poisons for those that love toxic yuri.

Stories include:
- **A Full-time Project** - an arrogant 'man' makes an unexpected discovery.
- **Box** - an old box in a neighbour's wardrobe has an ancient secret.
- **The Human World** - Zoey's life is a mess. But an offer from a businesswoman might improve things.
- **Tempting Poison** - in a futuristic brothel, an enhanced girl can be more dangerous than expected.

...and 9 more stories.

Printed in Great Britain
by Amazon